"Credo, ergo sum"

"Credo, ergo sum" explores the meaning of belief, faith, trust, and hope, in the face of dire circumstances. It comprises Volume II of the "ergo sum" trilogy which addresses modern skepticism of science, among other things.

Contents

Credits

I thank Terri, who read, but should have written.

Prologue

Michael Kerr and Leon Adamson were first to detect a beacon from an extra-terrestrial advanced culture in 2042, in the midst of Earth's global warming crisis. The overheated atmosphere punished both rich and poor, the poorest paying with their lives by the million. The United Nations sent Michael, Wendy and their children Colin and Andrea, with Ian and Wendy Cowling and their twin babies, 12 light years to the system of tau Ceti in the ship Nantucket. It was a mission of hope.

Eight years later, the two families found the beacon, and much more. They were to face a cruel and entirely unexpected reality. Their mission became the best hope for not one, but two civilizations.

Meanwhile, on Earth, ironic twists of fate helped to sow seeds of political change.

Chapter 1

Rosie

I re-entered the sealed port of the Nantucket, blinked several times to try to recover from the "snow-blindness" of the bright moon, and removed my vacuum-sealed space suit. Rosie had already made sure our teens, Colin and Andrea, were in bed. She was was working in the galley. "You look drained," she said, "why not shower and come to bed?" I was indeed exhausted, so tired, the events of the past few days had revealed the enormity of our situation. We had no clue what exactly lay before us, but whatever it was, we had decisions to make. A few minutes later, the tingling of the shower's hot water stimulated sensations of reassurance, warmth. However, this time they were mere distractions, unable to reach the knots of anxiety buried deep inside. When I had dried off, and laid down, I felt as if I had been up for days on end. Before this moment I had not understood the impact that the latest series of discoveries were having on me. I was dead tired, not so much physically, but emotionally.

Rosie approached with a warm glass of milk. I drank, put the glass down, and held Rosie closely, so close that she grunted in a little discomfort. She was my rock, wife, lover, mother of Colin and Andrea. A mother to our entire small world of eight, the four of us and Ian and Wendy's younger family. I yearned for Rosie's closeness, the kind that only comes from mutual love and understanding at times of need. I had been out on the inert surface of a dead moon. I was mentally still in the cold vacuum of space, and I needed her soft strength more than ever.

"I'm sorry if I squeezed too hard, honey," I whispered, "I really want you close to me tonight. I am not sure I will be able to sleep. Out there. It was, it is... utterly without mercy, our situation, our kids, the planet,..." She made her comforting shh-ing sound. Then she said, very gently

"We are not meant to carry these things alone, honey. Let me share your load. How about we have some chamomile tea and talk, but before that, let's watch the kids sleep for a few minutes." This was something we had done when they were very young. Colin, seventeen, Andrea, fifteen, had known only four adults and two babies, now children, in the past eight years of spaceflight.

I knew that we had been so lucky to have Rosie as the Nantucket's "therapist". The people who had decided who should travel, had made wise choices. I had not understood the need for families, especially children. But perhaps now, I was starting to. "You nearly always come up with the best ideas. I'll make the tea, then we'll watch the kids."

"Nearly?" she asked, smiling.

Colin and Andrea shared a sleeping cube, now separated by a soji screen. They were approaching adulthood. We moved their screen aside and sat under the 0.1g lunar gravity between the two beds. Their soft rhythmic breathing could be heard above the ship's life support system, a warm hum in the background. We sat for ten minutes or so. I could feel the knots in my shoulders and back release a little as I copied Andrea's gentle breathing pattern, and relaxed my back into Rosie's warm, massaging hands. The children had lived patiently with us inside the Nantucket for over half of their combined lives. They were remarkable children, not just because they were ours, but because we had, in teaching them, learned so much from them. I had to thank the person back home who had decided that children would be critical for our journey. The children had repeatedly helped us to keep our feet on the ground, even when there was none to stand upon. Literally and figuratively.

Afterwards, Rosie and I moved quietly to the lounging cabin area, and sat together to drink our nighttime tea. After lounging in each other's arms for a few minutes, in silence, Rosie asked

"How are you feeling, honey?"

"Right now, mostly OK, thanks to you," I said, "in ten minutes, an hour, tomorrow, I don't know."

"That's OK for now. You were out on the moon's surface for a long time, without communicating. What was going on inside that helmet of yours, behind the visor?"

"Are you sure you really want to know?" Without saying a thing her expression said "Oh, come on. You know me better than that!" I gave a small, nervous laugh. "OK then." I took a deep breath, I could feel my anguish rising. "I saw out there the folly of humanity. Looking out, under the light of tau Ceti, I saw the Sun, close to the bright star Arcturus, as a mere star, an ordinary little star. The Earth was there somewhere, dwarfed by the Sun's own light, that appears so modest from here. I saw so clearly how tiny and isolated our planet is, how precious it is. Out there on the surface, embedded in the lifeless void, I cried inside, because society had put its narrow self-interests ahead of the future of this extraordinary little planet, our home, our only home. As a society, how could we have permitted mere convenience and short-term interests to deny the future to new generations?"

In that moment I looked over to the planet filling the view through one the ship's ports, its atmosphere grotesquely bloated by the action of greenhouse gases. I wondered if our own myopic policies, our catastrophic decision to allow global warming, might be some kind of universal trait. After all, the evidence was right above my head. "Our individual short-lived comforts had spoiled Earth's atmosphere," I continued, "but we were not the first. I believe we were beaten to it by these locals, the Cetaceans, right here. We traveled twelve light years to seek their superior knowledge, and we have arrived only to witness a planet in a more advanced state of changed climate than our own. It's almost too much to bear." I took a huge gulp of air as I sobbed, and forced myself to continue. Rosie held my head as I cried onto her warm, soft chest.

"I am starting to think that evolution-driven technological advancement naturally leads to some kind of blind – at best myopic – collective indulgence. In turn that leads to global instability. Right there, on the planet above our heads, we have evidence of global warming, climate shift. With our Earth on the same track, I feel we have nowhere to go.

Even if global warming were not the most immediate problem, I feel we would have found another way to endanger our grandchildren. Just look at the antibiotic resistance..."

"I understand your feelings completely," Rosie whispered, "but I also disagree completely." I looked into her eyes, she was smiling, yet she was quite serious. I wiped tears from my eyes, wanting to hear something good, something positive, something to help me move forward. "Let's figure this out together. You're not going to sleep well without some kind of reassurance. So, let's have another look at what we *actually* know, shall we?".

"Alright then." I began. I tried an abortive smile. "Our situation here looks like we have failed, if we simply review the facts. We are twelve light years from Earth, sitting next to an abandoned but functioning alien lunar facility, our 'interstellar beacon of hope'."

"Now, I asked for facts only please."

"Sorry. OK sweetie." I blew my nose. "The kids spotted two small vehicles some distance from the facility, gradually losing power, empty. Tracks there show that the two alien occupants are together somewhere out on the moon's surface. Their host planet shining down on us has become a pressure cooker, the average temperature of 34 Celcius would not sustain our kind of mammalian life. We need water to return to Earth. Water is on the planet, but we may, or may not be able to reach the surface. That's how I see things."

"Very well. Those facts are clear. But you missed some important ones. We are all well, in unreasonably good spirits, Nantucket is in great shape with years of life support left, and we are still hearing from our homing beacon, Bishop Rock.

"It's really important now, at this special moment, that we believe in something, in ourselves, in the children. We may fail in our mission to contact the Cetaceans, to help us understand our global crisis on Earth. But do you not see that we still have options, so long as we can think, so long as we have hope?" said Rosie.

"Sometimes it's so hard. It feels so desperate out here. I saw our Sun suspended in the sterile vacuum of space, it is everything to us, but it nurtures a planet that we have chosen to set on a terrifying trajectory. I try to keep a positive face for everyone's sake. But I feel anger, sadness, frustration. How could we allow Earth... Sorry, but I am not sure I can keep up what feels right now like a charade, offering hope to our families."

"Those are all legitimate feelings, darling," she said, and I buried my face again.

I continued, quietly, "The situation here looks like it's 'curtains' for the Cetaceans, the locals on the planet above. I guess we know nothing of their biological resilience to a changed climate. But this 'Beacon of Hope', the laser station outside, now looks to me like it might be transmitting an interstellar SOS. Back home, the curtains seem to be closing in, too. Just look at the appalling consequences of the changing climate we have been witnessing from afar."

"And yet there is hope, real hope, I see it in you, it is perhaps buried deep right now, but it is there. Now, can you tell me what we might do, right here, tomorrow morning, when everyone is up? One thing at a time."

"OK, I can try." I stood, wandered around the room, took some deep breaths, freshened my face with a wash-cloth, and sat with Rosie again. "Right, as I see it we do have several options. We could, probably should, look for water in the childrens' scans of the moon. If successful, we could turn around and leave for Earth, our mission declared by us to be a 'successful failure', like they did for Apollo 13," I said grimly. "or, we could attempt to get Nantucket into orbit around the Cetacean's planet, and go from there. But, you said one thing at a time. Let me think..." Concentrating on the "here and now", I could feel a rising feeling inside my chest. "OK, there is one thing to do that I find most urgent, compelling even. I believe we should attempt to help the extra-terrestrials on this moon, if we can." Rosie smiled, I found myself speaking more quickly, I seemed to have gained a little determination out of my despair.

"Well, of all the many things you have taught me, Rosie, I think the following is maybe the most important. There is *hope* in humanity when we try to help each other, not just ourselves. And here and now I feel compelled to see if we can help someone, some being that is *truly* different from ourselves. I have come to believe that this is an essential quality of humanity, by itself this is almost the definition of hope.

Where would we be without this? The view of our Sun from this moon is crushingly depressing from one point of view - a view I would have held until we embarked on this trip - namely, that it is just one of billions and billions of stars. But from the point of view of humanity, that little star is everything. What I think I have learned is that from the point of view of the Universe, humanity is everything."

Rosie was still smiling when she said "That is quite the statement from an astronomer, scientist, empiricist,..." she smiled. But, what do you *really* mean?"

"Yes I even sound crazy to myself. But out there on the moon's surface, the literal, empirical reality is indeed one of a deathly cold vacuum of space. Those rare life-giving planetary oases are seemingly destined to be ruined by advanced civilizations. These feelings hit me really hard. But now, I am beginning to see a different reality, that of awareness, consciousness, emotion, conscience, kindness, love, hope.

"I ask myself, what place has hope in the cold, cold Universe? 'None', some might say. But hope must be the crowning glory of the Universe, for everything is meaningless without it." I embraced my clever wife, who had come over to me and held me from behind.

"I don't think you are as exhausted as you think you are. This sounds like a plan," said Rosie, her warm smile, "and you found your new hope by yourself."

"I don't think so," I said, "in any case it's not much of a plan, it's merely a start."

"But that is the most important part."

I could not help but smile at her wisdom, kissed her and looked into her deep brown eyes. I felt that a huge beast was being lifted from my back, I laughed a bit too loudly, nervous energy almost exploding from my body. "Shh!" she whispered, laughing a little too. As I held her I realized that the best teachers always let you discover for yourself. I imagined making love with her in the 0.1g lunar gravity.

A bump from the kids room. "Mommy, I had a bad dream, mommy, mommy!" said Andrea. She was "young for her age", in some ways. I could hear Colin groan, and turn over. I had forgotten to replace the screen.

"I'll be right there" said Rosie, smiling.

She was my guide, my teacher, shedding light on depths within my soul that I had avoided, had been afraid to explore. The deeper into space we ventured, with Rosie's guidance, the deeper I could look inside myself and see more clearly. Rosie, was not merely a therapist, psychologist. She was my guardian angel.

Chapter 2

Down the rabbit hole

Over breakfast, we usually did not talk "mission" stuff. But that day, with all the recent findings, we could not really avoid it. I was calm, rested, and thankful to Rosie for guiding me to the previous night's enlightenment. I felt as if I had emerged deeply wounded from an epic battle, but had been healed through the most natural of medicines - woman, mother, nature.

So, after clearing up, we had a more serious and directed discussion. Wendy was charged with playing devil's advocate. "So you want to go and find these aliens, these bipeds. None of us knows what you will be facing out there. To pursue these aliens so directly is a total gamble, a huge risk, God knows what you will find, if you can indeed find anything in the limited time available. If you are successful in finding them, and if they are in good shape and want to hold hands and skip back to the Nantucket, then what? We will have to host them in our environment here, or in their buildings, their 'Domes'. But they must have left the Domes for a reason. From what we can glean about the planet's atmosphere, it looks like they breathe oxygen, but we have no clue as to the flora and fauna they might be hosting in symbiosis. Imagine our gut bacteria being let loose on an alien world... If we are anything to go by, these 'Cetaceans' are hosts to myriads of bacteria and God-only-knows what else. Exposure to them could make the ebola virus look like the common cold for us. We cannot allow any exposure between us and the Cetaceans." We looked grimly at one another. Ian then outlined many other known dangers, mostly involving equipment failures.

"Indeed, it is a step into the unknown, something that, if we go, will require enormous faith," Rosie said, "we would be going into a very dangerous situation. But remember, we have come a damned long way, we are already at a place with limited options. I think we have to try to make something good happen, I emphasize the word *try*. If we do not try, then, well, I think we must consider our mission as a failure. If we do, it must be regarded as something of a success."

"I agree with Rosie," I said, "specifically, we need to have some meaningful goals, things we can fight for, and things we can believe in. Last night, Rosie and I discussed the benefits of taking one day at a time, right here, right now. Yes I know this seems trite, but otherwise it leaves us in limbo, a place literally between worlds, between the places that can nurture us and where we can live some kind of normal life. Rosie and I have to believe we will return to a normal life, we think it is perhaps not much further, emotionally speaking, than we have already traveled. While it may seem difficult for us to hope that we might make it back to Earth, all that way, we can easily see that we can make a difference, here and now. So, I say we go and at least try to make an immediate difference to those who appear to have asked for our help, no matter who or what they might be. This act alone is what separates us from the cold dust and rocks of the moon outside. I believe our 'friends' out there have asked for our help, and they really seem to need us now. I cannot help but feel that only good can come of it."

"Dad, and mom," said Andrea, "remember when we were talking about those special but ordinary people, the visionaries, the lighthouses, or 'fyrtårne' was mom's grandma's name for them. I think what you are saying is that we need to be like them. Like Mother Teresa, maybe. Remember that she put herself in terrible danger too."

After a charged silence, Wendy said "Well, that's hard to argue with, I don't think I can come up with a case against such thinking except for self-preservation. Hell, I never liked being a devil's advocate. I really hope that there are no risks to our self preservation that we cannot handle with appropriate care. I really don't believe that we will have to deal with mindless monsters on this moon's surface." One or two impressive sci-fi movie failures jumped into my mind here. I chuckled, to myself only. This was after all our entire future that was under discussion. "But if we consider only self-preservation, and do nothing, we will deny our very existence as sentient, compassionate beings. I am not interested in coming all this way to allow skepticism to triumph, I think we know where that will lead. I don't want to live on knowing there are two dead aliens somewhere on this moon, that we could have helped, never knowing if they could have helped us. I am not happy with that. And we will be preserving ourselves for what, without making contact?"

"So, moon walk it is, then?" asked Ian, after another long pause of wringing hands and exchanging glances.

"Get your boots on, Ian, we may as well start immediately, and it's your turn. Take Rosie or me, we need at least one parent here for Peter and Barrie. " I said. "Wendy, you are needed here for clinical preparation of the isolation pod." She nodded, and shot a worried glance to Ian. To de-fuse the situation, Ian asked

"Rosie, please would you like to join me for a trip down the rabbit hole? I believe it will be awfully interesting down there..."

"How could I resist such a charming invitation" said Rosie, feigning a southern belle accent and batting her eyelashes. We all laughed, probably because of the relief of making a decision, as much as the exchange.

"There are not any rabbits out there on the moon, are there?" asked Barrie. "I like rabbits, or I think I do, I can't remember touching one ever. But I thought they needed things like lettuce, and I don't think there is any of that out there."

"No dear, you're right, there is not a single rabbit out there!" laughed Wendy, "Or, at least we don't think so. I'll tell you what, let's go to the cube and you can look up some writing by a chap called Lewis Caroll, and you can see what daddy meant. It'll be fun."

Fifty minutes later Rosie and Ian exited the Nantucket, fully briefed. We had made up a whole new protocol, the manuals from home were now obsolete. I happily and ceremoniously deleted a manual entry entitled "The Unexpected: new protocols for new circumstances." We needed autonomy. Wendy and I had a good chuckle.

Chapter 3

Nicely undone

A few minutes later, we received a mail package of a hundred gigabytes from Bishop Rock, the station broadcasting towards us and the tau Ceti system. It was our "mission control". Such large up-links to us were easy, even across interstellar distances, but they were rarely this large. The yellow lasers at the Rock operated at frequencies that required only a blast of a few seconds to send so much data.

I figured I had about half an hour of dead time before things started to get interesting on the moon's surface. So I glanced at the news feed while monitoring the comms chatter outside the ship. "Rosie, we have a new news feed" I said, "or should I say 'old' news feed!" I often got distracted by the inanity of the English language- what is meant by "old news", and then, if that is satisfactory, what is wrong with saying "new olds"? I snapped back into the real world when I heard Rosie say "Roger that".

Still distracted, I thought again of the odd fact, which was simply that in the "here and now", the "now" transmissions from Earth now arrived twelve years later than they were sent. To us, that had to be good enough, we had to imagine simply that this is "today's" news, not yesterday's. Emotionally, we had not really gotten to grips with the notion that there is no "today" for us on Earth. There is only "today" for us "here", on this moon and the planet below, in our immediate neighborhood.

I was beginning to believe that "here and now" was a callously isolating expression, over interstellar distances. In contrast, global communication experienced by humanity at the beginning of the twenty-first century was essentially instantaneous. Wendy had remarked that she now understood perhaps a little of what Shackleton and his men felt in their extreme isolation on Elephant Island, only a century before. We had all studied those legendary and heroic voyages into the unknown at length. Who could not admire Shackleton's astonishing unwillingness to give up against inhuman odds? I knew I had little of that kind of spirit. But I did have Rosie, who did.

So, trying to think of this as "today's news", I listened to the usual greeting message, from my dear friend Leon.

"Nantucket, this is Leon. Good day, night or whatever it is with you. We expect that you have arrived safely at tau Ceti, or that you soon will. Congratulations if so. I wish I were there to see it all, but then I would not be here, with my boy!" From the video I could see that fatherhood and family life was suiting him very well. It seemed that Ria had unleashed some of the "normality" that had so obviously lain so deep that, when a graduate student, even the other grad students thought him quite peculiar. He was proudly bouncing young Michael on his knee, precariously. "We anxiously await news of the interactions with the Cetaceans, people here are very interested in the first contact, don't forget your protocols and manners, and don't forget to record everything!" So much for that, I thought.

"We have included in our latest package an auto-update of the motor system, to take care of the motor stability issues we have examined. Hopefully that will go smoothly and reassure you of the motor's reliability." I had happily forgotten about this problem. I swallowed deep and said a personal prayer to the physics gods: please let this random event fall somewhere outside of the next decade or so.

The "Archbishop", the unimaginatively named director of the Bishop Rock laser facility, stepped into the frame. "Thanks Leon. Hi folks, please enjoy the news programs immediately following this message. To commemorate your expected arrival and unprecedented achievements, we at Bishop Rock have made our own version of the news. No BBC or Reuters here, no attempts at unbiased reporting. We just hope that it cheers you all up. All the best."

I paused the program and pressed the comms button. "Rosie and Ian, something to look forward to when you get back- the Bishop and his deacons have sent us a special personalized news package, with 'news' in quotes by the sound of it. We'll get some popcorn in the kettle after dinner tonight."

"Nantucket, copy that, sounds good." said Ian. He sounded distinctly serious. I decided I should stick to the script and watch the programs only in the background. I checked life support status for the two moon-walkers, and scrolled idly through the news reels. Leon really looked like a good dad, I fast-forwarded through many minutes of father and son frolicking and wrestling, swimming, diving, fishing, playing soccer, softball. Ria was a darned good photographer too. There were kinder-garten events and graduation, first grade, birthdays, wedding anniver-saries. I became distracted by the old question of why had we embarked on this mission and denied this life to ourselves and our children. What price had we paid? I was tired of asking myself the question, and I knew there was no possible answer. But had we made a mistake? Why would this awful doubt simply not go away? I could hear bouncing around in the kids' bedroom. My "little Michael", Colin, was stuck here. Leon's younger Michael had all those school-friends. Our kids' entire world was eight people. But, well, they were happy, so far as I could tell. But that was what worried me, I felt sure I could not tell if they were indeed happy and well-balanced. I had to rely on Rosie, and Wendy, for that, and their position was always, "so far, so good". Fair enough.

I tried to snap myself out of these thoughts. Why did I keep getting so distracted? I was after all responsible for my family out here. I would have bet money that Shackleton did not have that particular problem.

The videos from the Bishop and deacons covered some 6 or 7 years, judging by young Michael's progress, from a newborn. Many were shot at the same places- the birthdays always occurred at Ria's parents' house in New Jersey. Our kids did not have grandparents. I noticed there were two consecutive years in which waters were lapping at the road on which the house was built. I checked to see that the years were indeed not the same. They were, not. The cakes were different: batman first, later Harry Potter. The NJ water was a permanent fixture, cars were scarce but boats were moored to garden trees and fences. This was no hurricane season, as I had thought. It was the ocean. Oh my

God, Ria's folk were facing the Atlantic Ocean and losing. There was no birthday cake to be seen at that location, in later years in the video.

In a sudden change, Leon came on to explain that here was a genuine segment of a newscast that I might find amusing. His demonic smile and raised eyebrows took me back to McDonald Observatory. I laughed out-loud. "Nantucket, I did not catch that" came Rosie's voice, sounding stressed.

"Oh, I'm sorry darling, I am just laughing at some of Leon's more charming quirks." I felt bad. "Is everything nominal out there?"

"Yes, we are well on our way now," said Ian.

Into the news frame came an image of a silver-haired clergyman outside an enormous modern church. The headline read "Nicely Undone by Changed Climate." The camera panned around towards the the eastern end of the church. It was missing, entirely swallowed by a sinkhole some 100 meters across, far deeper, and pitch black. The reporter began, "The altar and choir sections of this new one hundred million dollar mega-church in Colorado were swallowed wholesale this morning by a sinkhole. The Platte River is thought to be the culprit, as it responds to the changed climate and weather here. There is a loud roaring from deep within the hole, which has yet to be plumbed.

"We have spoken to hydrologists along the Front Range, from Fort Collins to Colorado Springs. Such events appear to be entirely unpredictably, unfortunately. One hydrologist from Boulder described it as "an Act of God". The enormous depth of the hole is a frightening new reminder of the uncaring way that global change affects everyone. The building, the flagship of the Very Reverend Nicely's popular Fundamentalist Church, is expected to disappear into the abyss entirely."

The camera panned and moved in to show Nicely, ashen-gray, tears falling from blue eyes that were looking skyward. The foundations of his church were being swallowed like a raindrop falling in the ocean. The commentator continued, "Nicely said it felt to him as if God the Father had no power over Mother Earth. To this reporter, it seemed that she was also shaking the foundations of the Reverend's faith."

"Nantucket, we have reached the confluence," said Rosie, breathing rapidly.

Bombarded by contrasting emotions I replied, "Nicely done."

"Nantucket, please confirm," said Ian.

"Of course, err, I mean Roger that, err, confluence. Stand by." Damn, I needed to get my priorities straight, this was getting serious.

"Dad, you need to get your priorities straight!" came Colin's voice. "I'll take over the communications, you go and take a potty break."

"But..." On seeing his determined look, I gave up, knowing Colin was more than up to the task. Seventeen he might be, but he also had eight years of working with Nantucket's subsystems on his CV.

Chapter 4

Twelve steps

Out on the moon's surface, Rosie and Ian reached the point where the tracks of the two bipeds converged. "Here we go, further than Michael and I went before." Rosie could hear excited trepidation in Ian's voice, it made her heart skip a beat.

Taking a deep breath, Rosie said "We should get a move on" rather louder than she wanted to. "We don't know how far we must go to find the Cetaceans, and we will have to approach with considerable stealth." Even though the Cetacean sun itself was down, the planet's large silver crescent softly illuminated the surface. The shadows were not sharp-edged, like on Earth, but the landscape reminded Rosie of a moonlit midnight walk on a first camping trip with Michael, in the light snows that had fallen on Utah. For a moment, even those two alien tracks before her seemed eerily similar to those, now long gone, many light years distant. She snapped into reality when she looked up and noted again the proximity of the horizon, and the low gravity. In front of she and Ian were these two tracks. Two tracks, made by some beings' children, some 'persons' children. She had to think, to concentrate, don't over-complicate this. "Come on, Ian, we have to do this, time is ticking away." She said.

A few minutes later, the tracks still heading straight, Ian turned and stopped. "Wait a moment, Rosie," he said. On turning, he pointed out that only the top of Nantucket could be seen glinting in the planet's light. "I have to see what we are facing here. Nantucket, do you read me?"

"Ian, we read you loud and clear, is all OK?", replied Colin.

"Yes we are fine. But I want you to sing something, or recite something, Colin, because we will lose your signal soon, line-of-sight problems. We need a continuous feed, and something to distract us might be a good thing."

"Roger that." said Colin, "Let me just bring something up from the library." After a minute or so, he said "OK, I have something that might be a good distraction, especially if you are out there for some time!" He laughed. The humor was reassuring, briefly. He began:

I was born in the Year 1632, in the City of York, of a good Family, tho' not of that Country,...

Both Ian and Rosie recognized these words. They were the opening lines of "Robinson Crusoe", a book we had read together some weeks ago, around the "fireside" that we often projected on to the wall. Ian and Rosie looked at each other, and both could not help but smile in spite of their critical situation. "Wow, Robinson Crusoe, he's expecting us to meet with a 'Man Friday', maybe? No-one said he wasn't a bright kid!" said Ian.

"Hmm. Too smart sometimes." Chuckled Rosie. "But he does make me think. If I remember right, Crusoe set sail in 1651. So we set sail, err, 414 years later. That's a cosmic and evolutionary blink of an eye. But Crusoe's island and our lunar island? They are, quite literally, worlds apart. How far would humanity progress, in 414 more years, I wonder? Given a chance?"

"Now, that *is* the question, isn't it?" said Ian rhetorically, and then a little more seriously, "For the technology, maybe the sky's the limit. But for our ability to handle such progress, that is something that I am certainly most skeptical about."

They continued with a little trepidation, the unknown was always scary. Colin's voice disappeared abruptly after just a minute's more walking. Stepping back just a couple of steps, he returned loud and clear. Such was the nature of line-of-sight, with no ionized atmosphere to bounce radio signals. That, and digital audio, which was either on or off. "Err, excuse me Colin, we just found our limit, please stand by but continue reading if you would." Ian and Rosie looked along the tracks, they seemed to converge to a point close to the constellation of Orion, at this particular phase in the moon's orbit.

"Whoa. Wait a minute... Did you see something?" asked Wendy, "A glint, a reflection, something along the tracks? I thought I did, but cannot be sure."

"I saw nothing, sorry Rosie" said Ian. "We can't go any further though, this is the end of this road together unless we find a way to communicate. I didn't bring a long flagpole for an antenna, that was a mistake."

After a short period with nothing heard but their accelerating breaths, Rosie said, "No, we don't have such a thing. But the key word you said there is *we*. If just one of us went, the other could stay and relay messages, it would be safe enough, I am sure of it." I heard this and wondered where she was going with it. Before I could pipe up, Ian said

"Genius" replied Ian. "Now the hard bit. Who's staying and who's going?"

"You're staying, of course. I spotted the glint, I lay claim to it!" said Rosie. I was not happy with this, but then someone had to advance. "You should take a few steps back Ian, to make sure you are well within the line-of-sight. OK, here goes."

"Rosie, darling, think of what you are doing..." I shouted into the comms link. But I could hear her motion, Rosie was taking bounding steps one by one, each one leaving a hollow feeling in her stomach. Every few seconds she could hear Ian recite a word from the Declaration of Independence. She did not know he also had a flare for the dramatic. At each one she replied "check". Another glint ahead, reflected light from the planet's crescent! But it was just too dark to see clearly. From something like 100 meters, about a dozen bounds distance, she stopped dead. Standing very still and focusing hard, she could make out something. Two suits, suited humanoids, one kneeling, one lying? Yes, she was sure of it. "Eye contact" said Rosie, her breathing so rapid, pulsing in her ears, she was almost painfully aware of the life forces flowing with her blood. "Eye contact, eye contact, eye..." she said, unsure if she were getting through the pulsing to Ian. She stopped suddenly. The one kneeling moved, adjusted something on the other, and began to try to remove the other's helmet. "No! No! Don't! Don't! What the...?"

"Rosie, Rosie ROSIE!" Ian was trying to cut through the panic. "Rosie-talk to me, slowly, S-L-O-W-L-Y."

A deep breath. "I'm..." deep breath, "I'm, err, oh God" another breath. "What to do? I don't underst.."

"ROSIE, ARE YOU OK? OVER"

"Yes. Yes I'm, I'm OK, but, but..."

"Rosie, Robinson Crusoe, Colin is reading Robinson Crusoe to us. Your son, your boy." Ian was trying get through by appealing to her motherly nature.

"Colin...Robins.., Robinson... Crusoe" she was slowly coming round, still gasping, shocked, frightened, still panicked. "Robins.."

"Yes, he is reading for us, your boy Colin, listen to me. So, for Colin and all of us, can you slow your breathing, and maybe tell me, me here listening to you now, what you see. That's all I ask. I am watching you, I can see you, I'm with you here, you do not appear to be in immediate danger. Just tell me. Very simply. Nothing has really changed, just your perceptions."

"Maybe, maybe, yes I think I can try." She decided consciously to take a pause for herself and her family, this was important, maybe the most important thing she could do for her family. Even for her bigger family, humanity. Her heart felt too big for her chest, "just adrenaline", she thought, "that is good, it's what's needed" she told herself, unconvincingly.

After opening her eyes again, she began speaking, "There are two humanoids 100 meters from me, they are facing away from me, from us, towards the horizon. Oh no! Oh God!" Another deep breath. "One of them has removed the helmet of the other. I can only think... oh God... that he or she, or it, is dead. Oh, no! I must do something..."

"ROSIE" said Ian. Inside him, the thoughts came fast. Oh God, what is she doing? I must keep calm, no point in moving, I want to help, but if I move I will only endanger.. But Rosie.. must help... what to do?"

In this short time, after twelve steps or leaps, Rosie reached the be-suited humanoid. The being, about four feet tall, turned, and looked up. Falling backwards in astonishment, the being let their hands fall from latches holding their helmet to the suit. As the helmet rotated to reveal the interior, Rosie could see the face of a little girl. Crying. Frightened. Terrified.

Chapter 5

Mother

Rosie struggled to stop her maternal instinct from immediately grasping the child and holding her close. My God, it was so hard not to reach out, to help directly. Any human on Earth would surely have understood a mother's need to nurture, to protect, to love. The girl looked so sad, so vulnerable, so scared, what to do?

Rose watched as the child's eyes grew wide, ignoring the rapid-fire of panicked shouting from Ian's voice. She said "It's OK, darling, it's OK," without realizing it. The girl then stood up between her dead colleague and Rosie, protecting. Before Rosie knew it herself, Rosie had instinctively kneeled on one knee and had reached out. It was a reach across the last of the countless meters, kilometers, light years that Rosie had traveled. It was only one arm's length and it was twelve light years. It was a reach of life across the cold dead vacuum of space, it was the offer of hope, it was humanity. Above all it was simply motherhood. It was just one moment and it was all moments in history. Rosie was simply aware of the present in this place. The "here and now". She was only aware of a small child needing help. Later, she was able to recall nothing of Ian's manic voice in her headset.

This one small child looked through her tears into one mother's eyes. After a few seconds that seemed to Rosie like minutes, with two small arms the girl reached across years, eons, light years, across the Galaxy. It was the bravest act of faith that Rosie had ever seen, or could even imagine.

Chapter 6

Child

Later, Rosie remembered little more of this event, or of the journey back to Ian and then to the Nantucket. It was simply the overwhelming nature of the "here and the now", she simply had to take care of this delicate creature. Rosie was all instinct.

She had entered the Nantucket with the girl in her arms, unable to see or hear anything but the girl who had collapsed a few seconds before, her face showing a deathly blue-gray hue. Without thought Rosie, fully clad, lay the girl down and copied the action she had seen on the surface. The helmet loosened with a loud rush of air. No choice. Life or death, here, and now.

"What? No! Don't! Hell no! Wait! Germs! are you..." This Babel of noise in her headphones, she could not hear. She only noticed it as it disappeared on removing her own helmet to see more clearly and try to help this delicate young "girl". She was beautiful, but she was terrifyingly unmoving, and a truly frightening color.

It was over in a second. No protocols, no isolation room, just life. Or death. We stood, waited, silent, looked and listened. Wendy stepped backwards at first, then forward, Rosie held out her hand to stop her. Nothing. Then the small right hand of the fragile body moved, it dropped to the floor. Then again nothing. We exchanged desperate looks, still no movement. Children were crying somewhere. Wendy moved with sudden authority and determination, and she brought over a sterile cloth soaked in distilled water, from the isolation pod. She looked firmly at Rosie, reached, and gently squeezed the cloth onto the child's forehead. The water ran across her face and neck. Applying a second squeeze, the mouth opened slightly. Wendy took a huge risk, she dripped water into the child's mouth, the child coughed, then inhaled painfully while her body spasmed painfully. We remained dumbfounded, minds and hearts racing. Would she be able to breathe our air? If not what could we do? All kinds of "what ifs" pummeled my mind as I simply watched this desperate scene unfold. My mind felt like I was being drenched, drowning under a juggernaut of a waterfall. I was petrified, turned to stone. I thought we all were perpetually stuck in this moment of insanity, a moment of non-sense. Rosie had emerged from the Rabbit Hole only to jump straight back through the Looking Glass.

"Hello, my name's Barrie, what's yours?" Barrie had not been crying.

The girl's eyes opened, and blinked. Her eyes were deep, deep blue. She breathed. She exhaled and breathed again. And again. We watched.

"Oh, you look sad, or frightened," said Barrie, "do you want to be friends?"

Barrie's absurdly simple question, in such a desperate situation, helped me to understand why we were sent on our journey with children, as families. We needed these children. We all needed these children.

Chapter 7

Friend

Children. It seemed to be coming down to the children. Barrie's question, childish, naïve, struck a chord within me which reverberates still today. The alien girl could not possibly understand her words, but that was not what was important about Barrie's action. It was instead important for us, the adults, the adulterated. We needed to hear, really hear what the children said. We would not have been here if our grandparents, parents, and now the "Climate Skeptics", had actually listened, and heard words of children through the ages. Hers was a very common question. But there and then it was for me a moment of revelation. The revelation of the entire kingdom in "Bluebeards' Castle", that blinding, majestic assault on the senses, once experienced, never to be forgotten. Like in Bartok's blinding moment in his opera, her question washed away irrelevances, it could not be ignored, it changed everything, for the duration. Period. Unlike the dark subject of the opera, Barrie's question offered hope when we, and our new guest, most needed it.

I could not help feeling that this question was never too naïve, never too childish. Would our global climate crisis had occurred if world powers were more interested in friendship than power? But adults are of course too sophisticated, too clever, too busy. Too often childrens' questions are the target of malicious ridicule, readily shot down by cognoscenti, politicians, power mongers, by everyone, in fact. Adults always seemed to leave the most obvious, simple, important questions unanswered. Barrie had captured in four simple words everything that was right, meaningful, good. She expressed the quintessence of what it means to be human, a life-giving warmth in the cruel, cold vacuum of space, that was, for us, always just three millimeters of steel away.

The girl blinked again, took more breaths, and tried to get up. Rosie smiled down at her, reached her arms under her, and lifted. She was very light. Wendy motioned towards the isolation room, and the two women and Barrie moved together to lay the child down. The girl tasted more water from the cloth, looked deeply into Rosie's eyes, then closed her own eyes, and went to sleep. After a minute had passed, Wendy began to assess vital life signs. "I cannot believe this, but she's not so different from us. God, what a beautiful creature she is!" We decided to let the girl sleep for as long as she needed. We would deal with things like nutrition when she awoke.

"You said there were two," said Wendy to Rosie, "two aliens, was the other a child too?"

"Not now Wendy, I'm sorry, the other one is, dead. It was shocking, I cannot deal with that now. Let's do what we can for this one, please, I'll talk later." Rosie took a huge gulp of air and tried not to cry, she was almost successful. I hugged her. She had returned.

"Oh Rosie, I understand, I'm sorry, it can wait. We have one life here that needs care, I hope we are up to it. We might need caring for too, you have put yourself in danger. But I have to say that what you did was right. This is enough, more than enough, for now. I am a doctor so I suppose she, the, er, girl, is my responsibility. But it would be wonderful if you and I could share the work, I will need the help. She needs the help. God knows what we will be facing here. My medical training might be more of a hindrance, who knows? I might end up killing the poor girl. So I want you to be with me in this, and just follow your instincts. That will be very helpful."

We did not know what to do at that time, except simply to observe the young body resting, breathing comfortably. Myself, I felt uncomfortable breathing the very same air, now tainted by alien breaths, alien microbes, although I dared not mention it. I found myself wandering aimlessly in the cabin, wondering what might be going through the child's mind, how her body was doing, how we might be affected by her presence, her alien biology, her symbiotic micro-organisms.

Amid this time of anxiety, the children naturally piped up. Having seen the whole event, and seen the new girl being put to bed, they were now excited to meet someone new. The young twins believed that the most pressing issue was that of finding a name for the girl. So, with little else to do except observe our patient and send a 12 year out-of-date message to Earth, we set the children to work. They came up, with a name each. Each child had then to explain their choice. In the end, the youngest, Barrie, who was 20 minutes younger than Peter, had delighted us with her name. It was to be "Luna". Yes, our friend had been found on a moon. But Barrie had found a famous whale, a male called Luna, who had been adopted around 1999 by another mother, having left his birth mother. There was no knowing our guests gender, or even if the question of gender made sense. The name Luna was suitable, being gender-neutral. So it seemed to me, at least. (I do not recall why this seemed important, given the circumstances, but it did, all the same.)

So we took a vote. Even the other children could not choose anything but Luna, it really did seem perfect. After the vote Rosie said

"Oh, that's a perfect name, how clever of you to think of that. And the rest of you, well done, well done indeed!" We then spoke to the children about how we would try to make Luna feel welcome, comfortable, among us. I secretly crossed my fingers, hoping that she, and we, would be in a fit state for anything, given the completely unknown pathogens we, or Luna, might be carrying for each other.

Rosie suggested that if all goes well medically, then upon our first real interaction, we should all sit, speak gently to one another. We could look but not stare, we would use slow gestures to make her welcome. We would hold each other's hands or embrace, to show we needed one another. We would drink some water, offer Luna some in another cup. We explained to our children that she had lost a close friend, or a relative, on the moon, that we did not know what had happened, but she would probably be sad, maybe frightened too.

We had no clue what we were doing. But we had hope, the important thing was that we believed in what we were trying to do. I did not want to think of the consequences of a poor outcome. We all agreed that we needed this child every bit as much as she needed us. As Rosie had told me, it is important to deal with one thing at a time, when you are in crisis.

God bless Rosie.

Chapter 8

Luna

Luna appeared at the door to the isolation pod, which was to be her room, some hours later, close to the time when we were usually to retire to bed. She had removed her space suit. She was wearing a one-piece Lycra-like garment. She was all of maybe eighty pounds. We were in the main cabin, and we moved theatrically to our pre-set, "non-threatening" positions. It felt very artificial. From the shuffling and artificial movements of everyone, it was clear we all felt self-conscious and awkward. Nevertheless, as planned, I sat with Rosie, I put my arm around her, and smiled. The others sat together in as friendly and relaxed pose as they could manage. It all looked horribly unnatural. I suppressed with difficulty a burst of anguished laughter as I mentally compared the scene to an audition for a family sit-com. I could hear and feel blood pulsing through my ears, and I was sweating profusely. Rosie looked at me in shock, I never did sweat like a "real man". But she did not shirk away, we remained together as our script dictated. I later recalled that she discretely wiped her hand on my jeans, why remembered this, I don't know.

We all stared hard at the small girl. It was impossible not to. Ian caught his breath in his throat badly and went into a coughing fit. Wendy stood up to help and knocked a pint of water onto the cabin floor. The kids started giggling as Wendy jumped to mop up, and spilled a plate of cookies. I guess the others were feeling as awkward as I, it was now turning into that nightmare audition I had envisioned. Oddly, I did not feel like laughing right then.

After an initial look of shock, and a step backwards, Luna stood still. Moments later, her lips slowly stretched to produce a gentle smile, or something that looked very much like one. With what looked to me like an act of determination, she stepped forward, gently and slowly took another cup from the table in front of Wendy, and drank deeply until the water was gone.

Barrie stood up, moved slowly to Luna, drank from her own cup and said, "My name is Barrie, yours is Luna, can we be friends?" Luna smiled, gestured slowly to a couch, Barrie moved to sit down, and Luna joined her.

Evidently I had barely breathed during this whole encounter. I let out a huge gasp, and everyone looked and laughed. I felt like I had turned purple, I could feel the heat radiating from my damped facial skin, my hands were still glistening.

Then Luna put her hands to her chest and made a soft warm, musical sound, a mix of recorder and flute, an exotic bird. "Koo-koo-rah." Barrie smiled, did the same and said

"Barrie."

Luna put up her hand, to Barrie's chest, and said "Koo-koo-rah". Barrie smiled and touched Luna's hand, trying to repeat the sing-song word in her own delicate soprano. Luna's eyes filled with tears. Then Luna stood, made a ballet-like curtsy, turned around slowly, and returned to her room.

Barrie's face turned from a bright smile to one of a child having dropped the first hot fudge sundae of the summer break. "What did I do mommy, what did I do wrong?" said Barrie, running to Wendy and starting to cry.

"I don't think you did anything wrong dear. I think, no, I am sure that Luna believes she has found safety with us, and she has had a very, very hard day. I think you did just fine, Barrie, you did better than the rest of us. I think she is your friend already." We all agreed and gave Barrie big hugs. Her worried look became softer, and she produced for us a big, toothy smile.

"Then I guess we should let Luna rest tonight, don't you think?" said Barrie.

Chapter 9

Credo, ergo sum

Wendy insisted on sitting up, taking the first shift in Luna's room, merely to observe and cater for any needs Luna might have. She also confided in us that she would monitor us all, for obvious reasons. The deed was done, we shared air, microbes, viruses and all. She had no clue what to expect, but it would be wise to look for something in everyone.

The rest of us had the usual hot chocolate, and we were, excited, exhausted, nervous, worried. We were all too energized for bed. Rosie explained that we had good reasons to be happy. With Wendy's interjections, after sending away the children and teens, we discussed the potential difficulties, grave difficulties, with mixing alien species. But the fact that we had no choice, that we were fine after several hours, and that our guest was also fine, was a very good sign. Eventually we retired. Rosie described to me what she could remember at the first meeting, I fell asleep with those images mixed with the thought that humanity, the rest of it, would have to wait twelve years to hear of this meeting.

Sometime in the night Rosie woke me in a state of agitation. "Wake up Michael. Wake up."

"Wha, what?" I stammered, confused. "Is Luna OK, what.."

"Barrie is ill, there's something wrong with her, Wendy doesn't know yet, oh Michael, what are we going to do, if it is something to do with the alien, I mean, with Luna? It must be, mustn't it? Oh my God..." I was fighting to get coherence out of my grogginess from the deep sleep. My confusion passed almost immediately when Rosie's words were finally registered. We moved into the main cabin to find Wendy analyzing a little blood and looking into Barrie's eyes, ears, throat. I blundered painfully into a table. "Michael, for heaven's sake keep the noise down, we mustn't wake the other kids now, not now." On board the Nantucket, none of us had suffered from any kind of ailment. The environment was sealed years ago, only with those bacteria and other microbes needed for us to live normally. As Rosie had said, it surely had to be some reaction to Luna's presence.

"She has a temperature of 39 C, she is going to seize unless we stop this. She is lethargic, becoming non-responsive.." She put the fever medication in drops under her tongue, and some relief came swiftly. She lay Barrie in a recovery position with her face angled over the side of her couch. She put a cold damp cloth on the little girl's head. "Her temperature should drop soon, but I have to find the cause. We had no bugs in this spacecraft except those within us, the 'healthy' ones. This has to be from Luna, the girl, something is very wrong. Blood work shows no white cell increase, her cells are all within normal parameters, she should be healthy. God knows where this fever is coming from. Oh God. There, the readings show that there are no detectable parasites, no malicious bacteria or viruses. From Earth, at least."

Rosie noticed something new, after Wendy had turned her daughter over. "Wendy, what is that discoloration on the back of Barrie's neck?" asked Rosie, "I don't think I have seen that before. Have you?"

"What? Oh God above, what is that? OK, I'm the doctor, but oh my Barrie, Barrie... the girl, the contact, infection, oh no, what is going on?"

Rosie stepped up in reassurance, holding Wendy's hands tightly. "Wendy, look at me. You can do this, this is what you went through all that training for, yes it is Barrie, your daughter, and God how we love her, but can you not simply look at it for what it is, some kind of infection, and do what you can?"

"I don't know, I can try. Well, let's see." She took a mental grip on herself, and began mechanically moving into action. "Surface temperature is 2C higher over this purple patch than the surrounding skin. It's an infection of some kind, very localized. Her skin appears normal other than this color. But it is close to the cervical spinal column, a meningeal infection maybe? Oh I hope not. I could prescribe something, oh, but the blood pathology does not support it. What shall I do?"

"Wendy, what about taking a new blood sample, this may be a very fast-acting thing, it won't hurt to take more blood, will it?" Rosie asked. I felt completely hopeless. Wendy shook her head, and then immediately picked up her pathometer to obtain and re-analyze a new sample from her forearm.

"Now we wait another 60 seconds," said Wendy, "her temperature is trying to hold steady, which has to be good. But, wait. Oh no. It is climbing again. Kids can withstand higher temperatures than adults, but she will seize if this continues... and the lethargy is worsening..."

"Wendy!" said Rosie, "Luna. Luna is coming over."

Luna surveyed the scene. When she saw the purple patch, she turned quickly and went into her room. Seconds later she returned with her suit. Out of a pocket she took a small vial. She moved to Wendy, put a hand on Wendy's chest and said "Koo-koo-rah". With the other hand she gestured for Wendy to open Barrie's mouth, and then to drop in a drop of liquid.

"Oh my God, I cannot allow this, I don't know anything about this stuff," said Wendy, crying, "Barrie's temperature is rising. Wait, the pathometer. Oh no, there is still no known or detectable pathogen. She is not going to make it if..."

"Wendy, Wendy! We have no more options here. We must have faith that our meager communication with Luna is meaningful. I think she was saying something about belief, hope, mutual trust or something. We have to let Barrie get some kind of treatment, or, or.."

After Rosie's impassioned appeal, Luna moved forward, held Wendy's hands firmly, and looked firmly into her eyes. Then, she let go, turned, and opened her own mouth, and took a drop. She then opened Barrie's mouth, and let two drops of the liquid fall onto her tongue. There was no immediate reaction of any kind from Barrie.

Ten minutes later Barrie was fast asleep, no fever, no purple patch. She was asleep, with an entirely alien medication in her system. But she was just asleep, not dead. Luna approached Wendy, "Koo-koo-rah, Wond-ih." She motioned for Wendy to accept two drops of liquid.

"We must have faith in each other, Wendy, it may be foolish, but I believe we must trust Luna until we understand her, I cannot believe, given the last few hours, that she does not know what she is doing. If I were you, I'd accept the medication," said Rosie. Wendy looked very worried. "No," said Rosie, correcting herself, "no, you are the doctor, we need you to observe and care, you cannot do this, not yet anyway. I will take it." Wendy shook her head but Rosie determinedly stepped forward, and took the medication.

Ian had been holding Barrie's hand, looking very worried. He said, "We must be careful to try to understand what is happening here, I am most willing to be next if you need another patient for treatment. I will keep notes on the progress of Barrie and Rosie. I would like to guide Luna through some video records to try to begin some kind of mutual understanding of clinical medicine." Wendy looked astonished. "I know, I know, we have a very long way to go, and I am not qualified, but maybe in this situation a teacher with unsophisticated knowledge is better than a pro? And Luna will be able to pick up a little English, perhaps?"

To avoid a distracting debate, for both parents had experienced a nightmare with their darling daughter and were still highly strung, Rosie interrupted, forcefully but kindly. "I'll stay with Barrie, we will be patients together". She carried Barrie into our bedroom. "Keep an eye on us both darling," Rosie said to me,"please bring cups of water for everyone, cold water."

"Of course." I said, happy to help.

Soon, the rest of us crowded around Luna, who seemed fully awake and quite remarkably well. We cautiously invited her to look over one of our monitors, and we began to work through some of the video material prepared over a decade ago at home. "Water, fire, earth, air; man, woman, girl, boy; plants, fish, food, drink,..."

Luna raised her eyebrows. "Drink? Food?" I filled up her cup with water, she drank deeply. Wendy guided Luna out of the main living areas towards the biopods. A minute later she returned, having plucked a fresh, juicy pear.

"Food" said Wendy. She took a bite, and allowed Luna to smell the fruit.

"Food" said Luna. Wendy gave her a pear, Luna bit, smiled, and finished the pear, core, stalk and all.

"I guess we'll find out how our biota affect Luna now...", said Wendy.

"Why did you let her do that..?" I asked, clumsily.

"We are too far along to worry about these things. If you think for a minute, you'll see we have no real choice. We are flying with our pants down and everything hanging out!" said Wendy. "It reminds me of my medical training days."

Some hours later, Luna was still just fine, after a couple of visits to our toilet. Following several visits to our bedroom to ensure the two patients were doing well, I became convinced that Luna had made slow but steady progress. She absorbed everything, said only what we said, until one image of a couple embracing happily appeared. Then she said "Koo-koo-rah", again.

"Friends," said Andrea.

"Trust," I said.

"Love," said Barrie.

"Love, trust, friends" repeated Luna, musically.

"Koo-koo-rah" said Peter, now awake, blissfully unaware of the situation, and smiling.

It was a few hours since Luna had treated Barrie. Both Rosie and Barrie were doing very well. "I think we should all take the medication from Luna," said Wendy. She motioned for the vial, Luna smiled, and administered the liquid.

"Trust is not an option" said Wendy. "Trust is our way of life. *Credo, ergo sum.*"

"*Credo, ergo sum,*" Ian repeated. "I trust. I believe, therefore I am. I like that. It rolls off the tongue nicely. Trust one another, here, and now. We should all trust that this leads us safely into the future, the unknown. We do have much to do."

The contrast with the Very Reverend Nicely's cynical motto could not have been clearer. "Dubito, ergo sum", it made me feel a little sick inside. I was glad, and a little interested, in Nicely's downfall.

So, in time, in turn, and in faith, we were all treated with the medication, whatever it was.

Chapter 10

Cape Hatteras

The next "day", everyone appeared well. The four children kept a respectful distance from Luna, who was quite obviously tired. After a remarkably short time, Luna communicated, in English, that she needed to return to her station, "Cape Hatteras Light" as we had named it before we had any clue as to its nature. She wore one of the children's space suits, her own suit being out of breathable air. Using sketches, we understood that she must return there to send messages to her home world. Seeing no objection if she were accompanied, she and I descended to the surface and skipped across a few hundred meters to the first of the buildings. One at a time, we entered the airlock, she used a simple sequence she had illustrated, on a keypad. Upon entering, she removed her helmet. Upon her encouragement, I did the same. There was a scent of elder flower, or something similar, in the air. It reminded me of summertime in rural Massachusetts.

Luna moved to a computer station, and beckoned me to join her. A video image of she and I appeared on the screen. Using voice commands the machine produced another image. It showed peaked mountains shrouded by thick cloud. "Yes" I said simply. She acknowledged. She smiled, and then took on a serious air. Her voice modulated tones, again like the imagined tropical bird. I wondered what a conversation, a party, a crowd would sound like. An image appeared on the screen. About a minute later, more 'children' walked into the screen's view. Their reactions changed from alarm to fear. But upon hearing a few of Luna's musical words, they seemed somewhat mollified, and their faces changed to concern. After she had placed her hand in mine, their faces suggested intrigue, interest. I then witnessed my first conversations of the Cetacean race, punctuated by the one second light travel time from moon to planet. Luna embraced me, I embraced her. First, there was silence on the other end of the transmission. Then there was chaotic conversation, smiles, and tears, and embraces, and joy.

I was excited, but I felt a little uneasy. My training for this moment stirred something inside me. I had to be aware, cautious, but friendly. Those protocols had been drummed into us, based a little upon the interactions with previously isolated Amazonian tribal groups. Something about the nature of the children's reactions made me uncomfortable. I began to wonder if I had witnessed a reaction to an extra-terrestrial encounter, or to the arrival of a rescue party. Before I knew it, I had blurted out "No, this is not it. I, we are not rescuers. That is not our purpose. We are only a few. It is we that need your help, not the other way around. We, we only have each other, we..." I realized I was talking to myself, but could not stop. I punctuated my irrational outburst with the simple statement, "this is not right."

Luna raised her hand to me, and proceeded to do something remarkable. She closed her eyes, grasped two sensors on the machine, and delivered a sequence of memory clips of her last few hours. The planet-bound group stood in silent awe, witnessing and sharing in Luna's rescue, her welcome into our families, her medical interventions, her new language, her new friends. I had no idea of what she had done, but afterwards I could not think of a better way to be introduced. The group simply watched, and listened. Luna had managed to clarify my absurd last sentences with an ease, economy and clarity that I found astonishing.

I wondered, "how in heaven's name does that work, is it mere technology, or maybe..." It was only then that I noticed a vague feeling of light-headedness. My vision and hearing began to feel like I was underwater, everything becoming unfocused and indistinct, sounds muffled and from all and no particular direction at the same time. I retreated from the conversation, and slowly layed down. I felt very tired, I felt good, euphoric even. I wanted to laugh, so I did. "How nice if feels to be so tired, I think I will just take a nap. Fancy that, a nap. On a moon. Around a different planet, with a little girl, who's mind can project things on to a TV screen." I thought. I giggled uncontrolledly.

The last thing I remembered was Luna's face, her bright blue eyes looking down as she fixed my helmet back in place. I heard voices, in the intercom. Rosie, Wendy. "How nice to hear from you," I thought, or I said, I could not tell which. I fell asleep.

I awoke with two amorphous and blurry objects looking down at me. Luna, Wendy. The hypoxia had really taken it out of me. Wendy gave me thumbs up, reset my intercom, and said. "OK big fella, time to go home now. It looks like you've had your fill. Just keep breathing, you'll be fine, but less of the snoring please! Now we know what to expect in the way of oxygen pressure on the planet, if we ever make it down there."

"God, I feel like I had a skinful of bourbon, or something" I said, staggering.

"Yeah, at the Bar of Hotel Hatteras" said Wendy, unimpressed. "No more science experiments without supervision, OK?"

"OK." I laughed, and stopped because of the terrible pain in my temples. Wendy just shook her head in disapproval.

Chapter 11

Insomnia

"It looks like you were breathing an O2 mixture at about the height of Mt. Everest," said Wendy over breakfast the next morning. "No wonder you keeled over, even the best climbers on Earth have to acclimatize slowly."

"Well, I don't remember keeling, but at 0.1g how much keeling can you do?" I laughed. "It was strange, but from what I remember it was a nice kind of feeling." I added.

"Well, if it were not for Luna, you would have experienced serious brain damage and perhaps even death," replied Wendy, "you were lucky. She is a very smart cookie." I replied that I had been unthinking, stupid. I would do better in future. Then I remembered the astonishing memory down-link.

"You don't know the half of it", I said, her abilities are..."

"Well that can wait." Rosie had taken temporary control of things on the spacecraft. "We have to figure out a way to accelerate our mutual learning of language, Luna is the one doing all the work."

"That is okay," said Luna. "I watch your data machine when you asleep. I think I speak, and understand, better, speak slow, slowly, please." We stood in astonishment. Adverbs. Those had already almost disappeared from colloquial English decades ago!

"Well, I guess that answers that question" said Wendy. "I bet she could learn Serbo-Croat in no time!"

"Servo-Kroatt?" asked Luna.

"I am sorry, I was joking" said Wendy. "It is another language, quite different from ours, difficult for us to learn."

"What is 'joking'? You have more than one language? Very interested," said Luna.

"Luna, Luna! You understand us and speak English!" Barrie was jumping up and down in excitement, nearly hitting the cabin's ceiling. "I'm so happy. How do I say I'm so happy in Cetacean?"

"Cetacean, is Earth language?"

"No, it's your language, silly!" said Barrie.

"I see. My language is 'Neh-Voo', 'I'm happy' is 'su-yeh-koo'".

"Soo yay koo" said Barrie, "Soo yay koo, soo..."

"Well there's another first," laughed Wendy, "I guess Barrie is feeling a whole lot better now."

"Barrie, she is find, finded, fine. She is OK. The liquid I give is a treatment for a, a, disaster, disturb, no, disease we have," offered Luna. "It is not for us large danger. I sorry for infect, infection, to you. I look over your cube for physiology, immunology, compare with ours. Human and my body have much convergence so is good, I believe, I trust."

"Luna, thank you, Barrie is my daughter. I am so thankful. Now, can I ask, without any hidden meaning, are you fully developed, fully grown, adult?" asked Wendy.

"Yes. I have twenty five of our years, of time for our planet to orbit sol. We are adulted at 15 orbits. Is it OK if I use orbit for our "year" here?" We looked at each other, it made sense, and nodded. "Good. We are little-r than human, but converged evolution is makes us similar. I believe. I trust."

We shared a meal, during which continuously marveled to witness our notoriously cumbersome and messy language come under the control of someone from another planet. As Luna learned, so we all pressed harder with comments, questions, but avoiding (by agreement beforehand) the loss of her lunar partner. The children were beginning to badger Luna with barrages of questions. Rosie realized that this surely was taking a toll on Luna, if Cetacean physiology was indeed convergent with ours. "Children! Children. Please. Quiet for a moment. Luna, would you like to rest? You look like you might be tired."

"Yes, I would. I miss my partner, I will sleep." She took her leave and we sat down in silence. We all looked at one another, we would be able to talk to her about her loss, after all. I thought I would leave this part to Rosie. So, we returned to some of our daily tasks, and the children set to work looking at images of the planet.

That night, I could not get to sleep. "I believe, I trust". The words from an alien. In Latin these are both "*Credo*". No matter the translation problems, this adult alien even thought the same way that we had come to. Maybe. Surely this was a startlingly good sign. I smiled to myself.

When young, I had no problem believing in pure coincidence. Recently, I was beginning to feel there was more to life than just a bunch of molecules obeying simple laws but which led to complex, emergent behavior. That picture was the inexperienced, or I should say, "unexamined" life of the physicist, in me. I thought that, after all, if there were things such as consciousness and conscience, perhaps there were also real meaning in something like hope, which defies a rational or "scientific" explanation.

"Michael, are you OK?" asked Rosie.

"Yes honey, I hope to be asleep soon, I want to think through some things from today though. I was thinking about consciousness, hope, and the astonishing developments of the past day, and how nothing in my training could have prepared me for this. But maybe you are tired, and would really like to sleep."

"OK then honey, yes I am exhausted. Let's talk later, providing that is OK with you?" I nodded. "OK good then. I do love you, goodnight".

"Goodnight, love you too." Within sixty seconds she was purring again, a lovely homely, warm, calming sound. She was right, she was exhausted. I turned over, sighed and relaxed. I turned again. And again.

My inability to sleep was becoming a very bad habit. I could not help my inquisitive nature, even in semi-consciousness. So I let my mind wander free. Sometimes this worked when sleep did not come, other times it just stirred me up more. It was a risk, but I decided to let myself think.

As a kid, I drove my parents to distraction, always asking "But why, dad, mom, why?" When a young man, I always seemed to see things in a certain light, I always wanted a rational explanation. I looked for answers from the cold, atheistic rationality espoused by such as Richard Dawkins earlier in the century. As I matured, though, I began to think that such rationalists, while I could not argue with their position, had more faith in scientific methodology and agnosticism than most theists did in their religions. No, I did not believe that life was entirely a question of "selfish genes".

I especially remembered a curious business discussed, but not resolved, in the 1980s or so. It asked the question of what came before the "Big Bang". Genesis has one explanation. But physics, as understood then, actually broke down since two of the very best theories of the universe needed to come together, but they did not agree. So you would think that physicists were unable to explain where we come from. Not so! Stalwart atheists had come up with an explanation of why our Universe exists. Something to do with black holes giving birth to new universes. We happened to be in one that generated us as well as black holes. So it would generate new Universes. I once made the mistake of asking where the First Universe came from, the answer was as incomprehensible to me as the old lady's famous defense of the flat Earth sitting atop a turtle. "It's turtles all the way down". The bottom line was that the scientific "stalwarts" had tenets of faith that they were going to adhere to, and damn the torpedoes! I think it was then that I decided that, for some, *science had become a fully fledged religion. Credo, ergo sum,* all over again?

You see, I tried to convince myself, science is, like the arts, a very human endeavor. It does however have to deal with sets of criteria for success that have enabled us to make progress using "data", things given to us by nature. Herein lies one problem of scientific rationalization: it leads to the need for faith, in science itself, for where did these criteria come from? Was it not simply trial-and-error? I could not easily see how to reveal the faith that seems to be implicit in science. So I imagined an after-dinner conversation at an Oxford or Cambridge college, as the port was passed in the correct way and the mutual stroking of mental egos was done in the accepted manner.

"But Reverend, your faith is entirely irrational."

"But that is entirely the point of faith, Professor. You too have faith, that your scientific methodology will give you answers to what you want to know. I for one am not sure that it has given you answers above and beyond a few very useful tricks."

"Don't be ridiculous man, you can't compare your blind faith with that of a rational man, someone applying scientific methodology with its reproducibility, based upon cold hard facts! What do you mean?"

"But don't you see that your methodologies are articles of faith? So far as I can tell, science is pretty much a laudable attempt to rationalize, no, to "method-ize" little more than just trial-and-error. Philosophers have searched for centuries, but there is in fact no absolute "Scientific Method". Important discoveries are usually made entirely by accident. So you see, the foundations upon which science is built are of human origin, just like my own faith. Where do you think these methodologies come from? The same place as the origin of the Universe perhaps?" The reverend smiled politely, sensing he had the upper hand. "Following with port, will it be Cognac or Armagnac tonight, Professor?"

"Faith is the willing belief of something that has no rational basis. Trial and error is a rational thing. I believe in that. Surely you do too. Armagnac. Please."

"Indeed, I use it daily. Trial and error I mean, oh and Armagnac too. I am concerned with such things as the spirit of a person, something outside of your methodologies, I believe. A jovial spirit. A morose spirit. A spirited chap, I see no way for your simplistic methodologies to comprehend such things. The targets of "scientific methods" have to be separate from such things. I am quite unsure that the human mind has the capacity to understand itself, and therefore it cannot answer the really important questions."

"So science merely illuminates the Universe with no understanding of purpose, and technology provides bigger and better toys and tools?"

"You could put it like that."

I had witnessed similar discussions myself, but these questions worried me, quite a bit. But no answers ever seemed forthcoming. So, on this night I decided this was too big an issue for me. But I did wonder what Cetacean philosophy might have to say about this. For now, I decided to think on that bizarre conundrum of existence, we exist because we are part of a Universe, but does the Universe exist because we are here to experience it? Surely not. "Cogito, ergo sum", said Descartes. I think, therefore I am. Does the Universe think? Surely not. Does that mean it does not exist? Oh my mind was spinning. These were not scientific questions, they bothered me a lot, but I was no philosopher and in my middle-of-the-night turmoil I tried to turn to more mundane matters. My thinking strategy was failing to help me sleep. I turned over, and focused on the soft purring. That usually did the trick, eventually.

Chapter 12

Convergence

But my need to sleep was confounded by my buzzing thoughts. I could not help turning to perhaps the most remarkable discovery of the previous day. The genetic "convergence" of our two separate evolutionary journeys on two different planets seemed utterly preposterous, literally incredible. It had to be a profound new observation. At least the professor and reverend might agree upon that. Maybe.

I continued. This new "fact" seemed to imply that, of all the ways that nature could have chosen to make chemistry out of physics, and then biology out of chemistry, it had chosen the same route in great detail. Even if you re-started a billion-billion universes, this would be unlikely to happen at random. No, this confirmed in my mind what geneticists knew decades ago, there had to be deep, simple underlying pieces in the construction kit of life on Earth. Maybe then this was true for *all* life.

The atoms and their chemical bonds were universal, the same everywhere. The mere fact that both we and Cetaceans evolved to a convergent solution to the game of life, only one rational conclusion seemed possible. The Universe was equipped with physical, chemical, biological tools, but together these could produce self-replicating molecules and organisms apparently *in an extraordinarily limited number of ways*. Again, this fit at least in a qualitative sense with my recollections from genetic studies.

I worried briefly about the diversity of life on Earth, which was indeed astonishing. I also remembered these "living fossils", examples of animals thought long extinct only to be dredged up off the African coast by a small fishing boat. Evolution was a tricky thing. I sought solace by remembering that diversity in species reflected the adaptations of the *same* kind of genetic sequences. The same basic bricks were cemented together to make all known life on our own planet. Perhaps this happened here too? It seemed not reasonable.

Then I recalled one more thing. Not only chemistry but also physiology had certain ways of doing things in order to survive. I remembered vaguely that a little eel-like species, called *pikaia gracilens*, survived a cataclysm that other types of organisms on Earth did not. Little *pikaia* was a progenitor of all the vertebrates on Earth! So far so good, some convergence is expected, then.

But bipeds? Human-like mammals? Was convergence capable of explaining that? Apparently this meant that given a mixture of elements of life- H,C,N,O,P and S, and a few others, with a stable enough planetary environment, then something like mankind seemed inevitable, even universal. But this must be crazy! If this were true, then all those stupid Doctor Who and Star Trek episodes had it right! Humanoids seemed to be it. If Kirk was to flirt with and, with luck, inseminate an alien, insane as it seemed at the time, it appeared now to be not mere nonsense. I must have been deathly tired. Captain Kirk? Surely the Universe was not reduced to such simplistic cold-war propaganda, epitomized by characters over-played by chronically hackneyed over-actors?

I felt myself start to doze. Then, just on the edge of sleep, there came a moment of enlightenment, or so it seemed at the time. An "Aha!" moment. With such a sequence of events, the end point of evolution across the Universe, with its very particular physical, chemical and biological properties, must in time always lead to beings like us, complete with flaws, selfishness and the need to propagate our genes.

That, apparently was as far as my musings on biology was going to take me, tonight. Of course, this discussion with myself was desperately incomplete, far more full of ignorance than knowledge. My "enlightenment" was little more than a faint hope when seen in the cold light of what passed for "day" on Nantucket later. Nevertheless, happy to come to this realization, I turned over, and thankfully let sleep take me into the warmth of Rosie's soft body and its rhythmic purring beside me.

Chapter 13

Here and now

Everyone gathered the next morning for breakfast. Luna appeared to need little sleep. She said that she had continued studying through half of the night. She had plainly mastered conversational English.

"We must talk about some things," she began, "let me begin, please, by explaining how my race arrived here, now." She described some aspects of life experienced by her ancestors. Her condensed history had parallels and differences with humanity.

Their early history was filled with azure-blue skies by day, coal black skies at night, sprinkled with bright stars. But she herself had rarely seen a piece of blue or black sky. "Our early ancestors used chemical energy to make life more comfortable, more... *convenient*, as you say." The amount and quality of energy they used were initially limited, like us, to simple burning and animal power.

"But then came a period of explosive growth, our 'enlightenment'. Universal physical laws were developed first through careful observation of moving objects on ice prevalent in winter, and in the measurement of motions of rocks through the air. Later the same laws were found to apply to the motion of the moon and observable planets in our solar system. These laws led to rapid mathematical and technological advancement, much like your Renaissance.

"I was born many generations after this advancement, after my ancestors had multiplied exponentially, their numbers almost unconstrained because technology and the environment could support such growth. We arrived quickly at an age where we could use the very strong energies associated with the atomic nucleus. Many generations had become comfortable consuming this nuclear energy. But tragedy struck. After two nuclear disasters we lost faith in our technology, and we resorted back to chemical burning for energy. By this time our populations had grown so that we consumed massive amounts on energy. Our planet's air became unclean, slowly, so slowly. It was hard to notice.

"Unlike our nuclear accidents, the chemical buildup crept up just slowly enough that many did not notice, or could choose to ignore it. It was so slow that not even two or three generations could see differences. Now we know that our ancestors took away the blue sky, the night sky, with uncleanliness. The problem was not carbon-13, but carbon dioxide. In place of the blue sky, the heat gave us storms, permanent clouds, wind, rain. The heat, this lowest of all forms of energy came from their machines following laws of the Universe. It changed our planet. Ocean rise, disease, cyclones, storms, pollution. We lost almost all land animals, crops, many trees. The tiniest, fast-reproducing organisms and creatures adapted under the environmental pressure. Bugs, yeasts, amoebae, all species adapted. Alas, we and the larger animals we lived with, could not.

"The image we transmit into space shows our highest mountains, fifteen orbits ago. The picture was taken from a high altitude balloon, because these mountains are far above ancestors' cloud layer, clouds never were seen there until our generation. These mountains are, in your measures, over 50 kilometers above our oceans. At the surface the heat, the heat... it was only a little warmer than before, but it changed everything. We were losing our habitable land and had to act. We sent our image in hope. It is a beautiful, tragic image, a cry for help.

Luna struggled as she explained how she herself arrived here, and now. "...So we are all that is left, so far as we know. There are now just sixty two of my race, in a subterranean haven. My partner and I were to run our signal device, our 'lighthouse', as you like to say. But here, we were out of food, sustenance. Our planet's weather did not permit launches of space vehicles for an unusually long interval. We just had bad luck, with the changed weather patterns. I lost my partner just before Rosie..." she had to stop. Barrie went over to her, hugged her. Peter ran to a water supply and gave her fresh water. We looked away, in respect. She needed a little time.

I remembered counting just eight individuals on the video link from the planet. I did a quick calculation. These amounted to over one eighth of what remained of the entire Cetacean race. In the tragic loss of Luna's partner, Rosie had witnessed the equivalent of the loss of the population of Japan from modern humanity! My sense of grief was overtaken by growing panic. What in hell's name were we to do now? I looked around the room, eyes making contact with Rosie, who looked away. Then I remembered Rosie's wisdom. We had rescued one soul. That was a damned good start. But my selfish worries were soon put in their rightful place. Luna recovered, and continued,

"I do want to speak of my partner, Dah-dae. I presented his essence, his core, his soul, to the Nursery, under the Three Fertile Stars, just as my ancestors did in times before the skies closed. I did this just before Rosie found us. He gave his life for me, so that I might live a little longer, in hope that I might survive." Another deep draft of water.

"Then came Rosie, and you know the story after this." She put down the glass, and recovered some strength in her voice. "I was lucky to see the Nursery, it brings new life, hope. I am one of only two or three of my race who have seen the stars. Dah-dae saw them. Indeed he gave his life for me. But he lives on. He returns to the Universe in me, through me, in a new life, within me. I am sad, yes. But I am also happy, if you understand me." We looked in amazement, I could feel us all wanting to try to help, to comfort, to console this innocent and beautiful being.

"Oh that is wonderful!" said Wendy, rubbing the tears from her eyes.

"What is, mommy?" asked Barrie.

"Luna has a baby, inside, darling."

Later that evening, Rosie explained that Luna had been turned toward Orion on their first meeting. The Orion Nebula, a nursery for stars. A very fertile womb. I had observed this region, though visible to the naked eye, with big telescopes. It was a remarkably beautiful region, full of dust, gas, intensely new, violet stars, vibrant with energy embedded in delicate wispy plasma whirls.

Later, as Rosie and I relaxed together before reading in bed, Rosie said softly, "So the Cetacean ancestors had extinguished stars from their skies," she said. "I also think they had unconsciously extinguished the life and hope that was embodied in Luna's prayer to the Universe, for her partner."

We talked a little more. Back home, humanity was extinguishing stars, and lives. But here was Luna, partner lost, yet she was carrying hope. We had rescued two souls, not one, after all. "Luna, and her new hope," said Rosie, "that is a lovely way to say both 'a good start' and 'a good night'".

We snuggled tightly. Rosie made up a bed-time story for me, on the spot. Do you want to here one about "Witches or Wizards?" she asked. I fell asleep just after the "benevolent" witch had saved the pregnant beached whale, by conjuring up the waters of the incoming tide.

Chapter 14

Amazon

During the night, we found we had both awakened. Frustrated by this, Rosie and I simply had to talk more. We agreed that our original mission directives were eminently sensible, and now completely irrelevant. We had started a new plan of our own, of a different kind. Rosie believed that our next step into the unknown was to talk to Luna with the goal of attempting a planetary landing. Surely she had a way to return from the moon to her people? Intense, long-lasting violent weather had previously stopped supplies from reaching the moon. But we felt that, at the very least we should try to return Luna to her home and try to acquire the water needed for a return journey. This would be our next step, we would need to look at the weather in the new seasons ahead. But much, much more seemed potentially to be within our reach. Many unproductive questions were passed to and fro, until Rosie finally said

"Honey, I'm sorry, but I am physically tired, and this discussion is too stimulating for me. It would be OK if we could reach some meaningful decisions, but we have not. The good thing is that we know what we will do first, that there are options for us, even though we are years from Earth. We are on our own, we can and must make our own decisions. But right now, I need to un-clutter my mind, I think we'll do well if we take the plodding approach, one step at a time. Let's remember that what we need most is for all of us to have something to believe in. Some hope, in the face of unknown challenges. Let's care for each other's needs, focus on what we can do for each other, including of course Luna, and we will find a way to make a difference. I feel sure of it."

"When you say it like that, I can easily believe it," I said. She looked over at me, I could see the warmth in her eyes, and I melted, I could never resist that look. I moved on top of her, at 0.1 Earth gravity, it was an exquisitely tender contact. It made us slow everything down, and we made gentle, quiet, intense love. It was a true and honest re-connection to nature, to the Universe itself, a gift to humanity beyond understanding. For me it was a touchstone for reality during one of the increasingly unreal moments in my life. Afterwards we slept peacefully in the knowledge that one decision had been made, and that the others would surely agree.

Andrea woke us early, with tea and a string of indecipherable but musical noises. She smiled and repeated it. "It's Luna's language, she was teaching me," she beamed, "it's hard but not that bad really. I said 'good morning mom and dad'".

"Well, darling, good morning to you," said Rosie, followed by a re-markable yawn with maniacally disheveled hair. Low gravity, sleeping, minor acrobatics and electrostatics can lead to very "interesting" hair days.

"Mom. Your hair is like a clown's! Haha! Oh, and Luna wants to go home, to her home, to her friends." Ignoring the laughter, Rosie yawned and replied

"Yes, darling, we thought she would."

"She has a way to do it but needs some help," said Andrea.

"OK, that's excellent sweetie, but can we talk over breakfast?"

"Yes, I guess so. Don't be too long. With your hair, I mean," Said Andrea, still chuckling.

"Honey, just how bad is it?"

"Positively Amazonian," I quipped, "just like our activities last night." She poked me in the ribs, but at least had the decency to laugh.

Chapter 15

Transfer

Breakfast done, we began to discuss the next steps. In orbit around the planet was a station used by the Cetaceans for staging, refueling, resting and for laboratory work. Without machine shops on this moon, we would not be able to dock, but we could hope to transfer between Nantucket and the station. The catch was we would have to use very risky space-walks. But it seemed, after some discussion, that we would have no choice. The station hosted self-contained chemical rocket ships for transfer to and from the surface. Luna apologized that, without significant work, these vehicles could not accommodate human adults. We thought this of little consequence until she requested that two children accompany her to the surface.

The adults looked at one other with deep concern, what could this mean?

Her reasons were two-fold. First, her friends on the surface deeply wanted to study our physiology and DNA in depth, so someone would have to go. Second, they simply wanted to make contact, physically. In anticipation of many of our questions, Luna translated from a ground transmission containing everything important to know about the ground conditions, technologies involved in these "studies" of our children. They would use non-invasive low-power scans, painless blood-work, and children would spend minimal times actually under physical examination. Next, we asked about the shuttles. The transfer rockets had zero failure rate in more than 1000 flights, solid surface landing with retro rockets, almost no risk of straying off course or any physical damage, once the weather calmed to an acceptable level. This was technology tried and trusted, the weather would be closely monitored and success, more or less, guaranteed. In the end we realized (or rationalized) that we only had to decide if we felt that the goal of this was a good thing.

"Obviously we need to contact and engage with these people any way we can," said Rosie, "while there's always a risk in space, I think that our DNA may indeed be one gift we can freely give, as well as knowledge of our own physiology. Wendy has transmitted our medical database to them. But it makes sense that they use their own machines to measure our genetic makeup and other properties, to make sure that there are no "errors in translation" in something so important. Also, it seems their diagnostic methods might be more penetrative than ours, less invasive, and their imagers appear better. They see a benefit to us too in scanning us, their medical technology is in advance of ours, and we ourselves could well see remarkable advances for us in the long term. Perhaps more importantly, I believe we stand a chance of making enormous breakthroughs in some of the non-medical, psychological research, what makes people and society make certain decisions. Wouldn't it be wonderful to use the shared knowledge to understand how we might help save *two* civilizations from oblivion? So I say yes, hell yes! Let's send at least one of our children down, provided of course that they agree."

The kids were listening outside of our pod. "Let it be me mommy," piped up Andrea.

"No, me" said Colin, "I'm older and so I should go."

"We have not decided yet that ANYONE except Luna will go," said Rosie, "so hold your horses both of you. Wendy, Ian, what do you think?" I had to laugh, from "hell yes" to "hold your horses". Outside was the vacuum, instant death, an utterly alien environment. Inside was the comforting irrationality of family life.

After an hour or so of heated discussion, it was decided that Andrea and Peter were to descend to the surface, provided each kept healthy over the next few days or weeks. We would together fly Nantucket from our landing site on the moon to the space station. I had persuaded Colin than he was needed to handle the communications during many delicate upcoming maneuvers, it was really an important job. But he went to his room in petulant mood, to recover by himself, or, more likely, just stew.

Some ten days later, we were ready for a launch. At least there was no weather on the moon, we just needed to make sure our orbit calculations were correct. The transfer launch and maneuvers were of course controlled by our on-board computer, through the artificial and saccharin-sweet voice we had come to know as "Silky English". The computer was fed with orbital and other data from Luna's colleagues on the surface. I noted this in the log as the first time humanity had trusted "alien" data in developing a flight plan. As a footnote I added that we all believed that they had much to gain from our maneuvers, in case this might cause anxiety if the logs were ever read back home.

We left the moon under a combination of main motor and chemical booster power. As we accelerated from the moon's surface, the story of our arrival and then rescue of Luna, recorded by our footprints, was partly erased by the engine exhaust. But tell-tale signs of the first meeting between our civilizations remained, farther from our launch site. Perhaps, like Aldrin Base, these records would later be protected for posterity. The domes, Cape Hatteras, remained visible for some time. The first solid ground under our feet for almost a decade was now far behind. "I'll miss the gravity," said Wendy, "at least for a while."

A day or so later, Luna's planet had become slowly but surely bigger through the Nantucket's ports. The orbital insertion burn occurred in shadow of the sun and out of direct contact with the Cetaceans on the surface. Their communication satellite fleet was in serious disarray, and ground communications were not even attempted. We emerged from shadow and brilliant stars some ten minutes later, lit by a brilliant bluish flash of sunlight through the planet's bloated upper atmosphere. As the Nantucket rotated slowly, an immense structure – the space station – took up half of the sky, glinting brightly through the port. I was amazed at the sheer scale of the engineering involved.

"Fine orbital insertion maneuvers have begun. They will finish in 2 hours from now," said Silky English, "but we will perform micro-force maneuvers to keep abreast of the station". "Abreast?" I thought. Something would have to be done about that voice, it was getting a bit too human. But the computer would have to continue to trim our orbit to match exactly that of the station before we could proceed further.

During the long periods of relatively slow flight towards the planet, I reflected that the ability to handle such orbital problems was often called "Rocket Science" back home. It was still highly revered, unlike "climate science", I thought. This realization produced a bitter taste in my mouth. I tried to rationalize why this might be. "Elementary" problems in dynamics, motions of one or two bodies, had been solved by Isaac Newton. Several-body problems (like the motion of a space-craft under the influence of planets and a central sun) are solved by the same equations on a computer. These were apparently "respectable." But these problems are actually engineering, they are of limited inter-est to scientific research. Climate and weather belong, like many other areas of modern research, to classes of problems in "complexity". Non-linear effects lead to unpredictable consequences including sensitivity to things like butterfly wings, or the chaotic orbits of planets in multi-ple star systems. Apparently some such scientific problems warranted extreme skepticism, at least from those who find the answers "incon-venient". But these skeptics liked the convenience of scientific research on other complex systems well enough, such as immuno-therapy, when it suited them.

These were my still unresolved feelings, for what they were worth. But I remained saddened by the fact that the Earth's animal and hu-man populations were paying so much for the convenience of affluent people and their unabated consumerist agenda.

The next day, Rosie, Wendy, the two children and Luna, tethered to each other, made a slow transfer to the station. From the comm-link, it seemed that they were having fun.

"Whoa, just look at those stars, I've never seen them like that...". She was looking towards the Galactic center.

"Not now, Andrea, keep words only for maneuvers, this is very dan-gerous, wait til later OK?" Rosie's voice was strong, confident. But Ian and I were secretly terrified. It was decided that they should go all at once, not because of any technical reason, but simply that we felt we should attempt this as few times as possible. It went smoothly, as planned, but I at least could not ignore that half of humanity in this part of the Galaxy was out there, stuck between two enormously massive objects, on pieces of string.

"Are you having trouble breathing properly, Ian, or is it just me?"

"You mean, am I that stressed? Hell yes!" He responded, choking on his own spit, and having a coughing fit. We laughed, and it helped to reduce our stress a little. It dropped a whole lot a few anxious minutes later. Once the group was safely docked, the atmosphere on Nantucket seemed a lot less charged, suddenly a lot more breathable. We received the "all systems nominal, we're all OK, this ship is incredible!" message from the other side. The video feed did show a seemingly endless tubular "corridor" surrounded by all kinds of structures.

Rosie and Wendy were there not only for moral support, but they also had significant research work to do on the station during the surface mission.

Silky English then maneuvered Nantucket to an orbit with an average and safe 5km distance from the massive station, which now filled perhaps a quarter of our sky, the planet filling half as well. The youngsters slept with their moms over on the station, and with their dads on Nantucket. I doubt the parents slept much, I certainly did not. I was glad to have Colin next to me. The one thing I tried to remember above all was the confidence that Luna had instilled in us. There was truly nothing about her that gave any cause for worry. I could think of few on Earth about whom I could feel this way.

We had plenty of time with not much to do. While making yet more coffee in the micro-gravity environment, I contrasted the trust we showed in Luna, and vice versa, with by the shocking of the lack of trust between not individuals but entire groups and nations back home. How come it was so easy to trust Luna, the Cetaceans? Was it that we were simply in a situation that demanded trust? I did not think what was the whole story. No. The fear induced between different people and peoples back home seemed to take time to build up. Would this happen between us and the Cetaceans?

I wondered where this trust of Luna came from. Could I even trust myself, my *own* judgment? Was my trust in Luna, by itself, a cause for worry? I did not know a single human that did not have at least some problem, even Rosie had her moments... and then I remembered

Rosie's retelling of The Meeting. Why should we trust Luna if she had really given up all hope, and tried to remove her own helmet? Surely she knew then that she was already with child? Then what did that mean? Was she completely without options back in the Domes? Or was she so utterly shattered by losing her partner that she had given up hope? How could I let my only daughter ride with someone who could lose hope, to the surface of a different, dying planet? Was I losing touch with reality? But our reality was pretty much like going down the rabbit hole...

God damn it. Why could I not stop my mind from asking unanswered, even unanswerable questions? Then I was interrupted, thankfully, by Colin.

"Dad? Are you awake, dad?"

I started with the unexpected voice. "Err, yes Colin, are you?"

"Yeah. That's a dumb question, you're not as funny as you think you are. But could I read a bit to you? I never did get far into Robinson Crusoe, everything got a bit complicated after mom came back from the moon-walk with Luna. And right now, I just can't get to sleep. I wish I could have gone to the planet. I would have liked that."

"I have a feeling you will quite soon, and that your presence there will be important. You really have grown up a lot recently, I'm proud of you Colin." I gave him a big hug. He welcomed it and settled close to me. "I would really love to hear Robinson Crusoe, I really like those classics, the connections to home, to our roots. But could you start at the beginning again? No, that's OK. I think I remember, just start from where you left off."

"Thanks dad, you and mom are really great."

He started reading. I wondered if Rosie were getting a story tonight. Colin's voice was perfect for the story, deep and soft. I thought again, where would we have been without Colin, without all these four kids? They were the embodiment of hope. In this belief I knew I was not and could never have been able to gamble away my kids' future like those damned "Skeptics" back home. No, I was not going to waste time and energy thinking more of them. If I believed in one thing and one only, it was that we would succeed, must succeed, for the kids, for Rosie, and now for Luna.

"Credo, ergo sum"

Indeed. With this kernel of determined hope I was finally content with our decisions, despite the obvious risks to my family. I think I feel asleep before the end of the third or fourth page of Colin's gentle reading. I was reminded briefly of the same warm feeling from readings from my dad, many years ago, in time, and space.

Chapter 16

The Nicelys

The next morning, Ian and I awoke feeling somber. Wendy and Rosie had rested well, and were quietly being introduced to the station's main operation protocols by Luna. While they could read nothing on the computers, Luna assured them that on the planet her colleagues would be working on translation software. The two children on the station were, however, alive with anticipation of a possible trip, it was as if they were to go to a new adventure theme park. Colin and Barrie merely expressed hunger, so Ian took it upon himself to make a "proper" breakfast. During preparations of synthetic scrambled eggs, toast and hot sauce, Silky English said "Pardon me, everybody, there is a new transmission from Bishop Rock, would you like me to play it now?"

"Oh, yes, please do" said Wendy, slightly surprising us over the intercom. We decided we had to maintain an open line to the station while we were "here", and they were "there". The transmission began:

"Good day to you all, we at Bishop Rock eagerly await your latest news, the last time we heard from you, the Nantucket had far to go before reaching your destination," said Leon, looking a little disheveled and with a few days of beard growth. "Though by the time you hear this I should say, congratulations on reaching your goal!" continued Leon, with great gusto. "So, anyway, we are all well, young Michael has been-a-learning a few tricks." A video showed my namesake juggling three balls while balancing on a soccer ball, singing ring-a-ring-of-roses. We laughed raucously.

"Leon should have gotten hisself a dawg!" said Rosie, "but at least

Michael jnr. is not wearing a tutu, and I suppose that trick *is* pretty impressive." We had a good chuckle.

Leon continued: "Also, some really great news. Ria is expecting a little sister for Michael, and guess what her name will be, Rosie?" Rosie looked delighted, we hugged. "It will be Ria... No, just kidding, it's Rosie of course!" Typical old-time-Leon. From Nerd to clown without passing through normality on the way. "We are really excited, the time was up in the freezer for my little swimmers, and we thought we would like another baby. It worked on the first try! Those swimmers and Ria's eggs sure make a potent team, apparently."

"OK then. Well, apart from us, we are all eager to learn what you might be finding there. We are anxious to see how you are received and to learn from your experiences with the, er, alien beings. It's strange how we can be anxious about something we don't expect to hear about for another twelve years.

"Anyway, the news here is not much changed, except there are glimpses of re-growth of communities driven from coastal and extreme weather regions. Much of the Kansas tornado belt had to be abandoned as daily tornadoes decimated all infrastructure: farms, communities, schools. Initially they re-built some houses and schools, but the re-placements were gone within a year. The old tornado belt regions are pretty much continuous maelstroms these days. It is a steep road for us all to climb. We are all still consuming too much energy, far too much from carbon. We missed the boat on that around the year 2000. There is now an ugly-looking hard core of "live free or die" groups that is in-creasingly defending its right to consume what they like, no matter the consequences. These groups amount to about one quarter of the popu-lation of the USA, with somewhat smaller fractions around the world. I guess the USA is the world's flagship for "individual" liberty over col-lective liberty. There have been skirmishes around some live-free hold-outs in certain cities within the USA, with the live-free-ers taking over the city of Las Vegas. They are perilously close to the large Air Force base there, so we expect things to get nasty sometime. The Supreme Court has forbidden the Feds from moving in, using some clause buried in the bill or rights somewhere. So Las Vegas remains in a kind of feu-dalistic state led by a "board" of hotel, casino owners, police chiefs and others with their fingers in the Las Vegas tills Many people have left Las Vegas and other cities to stay with family where they can. It is very unstable. At present there are live-free check points at all entry and exit points to Las Vegas. Commerce seems to be working there, and there remains enough trading and gambling for people to live. Many wonder about what will happen if some group switches off power or water to Las Vegas, we feel it must be just a matter of time."

"This was to be expected," Ian said, "it really puts our situation here in perspective." Colin had written a nifty little program on the computer that would pause our playback while someone spoke. Ian continued, "Things are getting very scary back home. On the plus side, this shows us how important it is for us to get our story back, even to get back ourselves. What was it that Wendy told us? *Credo, ergo sum.* We now have a lot more reasons to believe."

Leon then continued, no longer held up by Colin's coding, quite naturally. "Michael, your friend Nicely seems to be, how shall I say it, experiencing a 'Second Epiphany'. In fact, he has gone underground, protecting himself from his previous 'investors'."

Leon proceeded to explain the astonishing turn-around for the Very Reverend himself. The natural demise of his mega-church led to a self-reexamination of such depth that he "defrocked" himself, he was no longer even a reverend. Some months afterwards he renounced his entire religion, dog-collar, plush suit, lifestyle, most of his family and all! After some rather unfunny jokes from the Bishop's end, Leon returned to the main theme. Apparently, and amazingly, it later transpired that Nicely and his son, Jimmy Jnr., or "JJ", had flown to Bangladesh on a privately commissioned Hercules transport plane. Both had emerged, heads shaven, wearing simple brown habits, among a small local crowd at an airstrip maintained by Medicins sans Frontiéres. No-one except a French doctor and Spanish nurse knew who these two peculiar characters were. The crowd pushed forward as the transport was unloaded, amazed at the apparent generosity from an entirely mysterious source. A BBC team happened to be in the area. News traveled fast. Against the will of the local gaffer, a trainee reporter traveled to see what was going on. The locals seemed to think it was an unscheduled drop, one of many, from established charities. The young reporter reported merely that a "young monk and his father" had delivered one of the most valuable cargos yet received, with medicines requested by the MSF local group. These donations were made anonymously, the BBC would try to pursue the generous patron.

At the same time, three other deliveries were being made in other affected and desperate lowland areas. For a short while the BBC did not identify who or what they had recorded. It was seen mostly as a curiosity for two minutes on the World News, and then forgotten, among the noise, chaos and calamities in the more spectacular daily news items.

But then, similar deliveries were repeated worldwide the next week, and the next. Intrigued, a BBC editor in London requested that the New Delhi office look at these deliveries in Bangladesh a little closer. The medicine came from suppliers worldwide. The aircraft also were privately commissioned using money laundered through a Swiss bank account. A young man in the New Delhi office had tried to get information from the MSF people, who had only agreed to accept the medicine if they acceded to the request to disclose nothing, ever, of its origin. They dare not reveal their source for fear of losing those critical lifeline supplies. The young man remembered the two monks. Using the rather poor images at hand, he made a search for face recognition. The younger monk showed up nowhere, he was out of the public eye entirely. The elder monk had several hits in Europe and the USA. One was a very right wing spokes-person for the fossil fuel industry in the USA. The young Indian proceeded to examine details of other hits, eliminating them one-by-one, aided by well established image processing techniques. After some hours of frustration, he returned reluctantly to the right wing spokes-person, as a possible match, absurd as that seemed. He found that the software simply could not eliminate him as a match. Statistically, there were only fifty or so possible individuals on the planet that could be a match. "James Nicely, Very Reverend, Archbishop. Public spokesman for right wing groups in the United States." The young man then had the idea of looking at some personal photos of this character, to try to get a yet clearer measure of the statistical match. His Editor in London gave him clearance to request data from a more personal and (theoretically non-existent) database, from Whitehall. Within a couple of hours, images arrived on his desktop. The first picture seized his attention. Father and son. The two monks. No doubt. All doubt gone, a few hours later, the BBC World News reported the scoop.

"The benevolent monks of Bangladesh have been identified by Rash Singh, our BBC correspondent in New Delhi. They are the Very Reverend James Nicely and his son, also James, known as JJ. Nicely, known for his public and eloquent denials of anthropogenic global warming, seems to have become a benefactor for those in the most dire situations, following the collapse of his mega-church in Colorado earlier this year. The BBC has been unable to track down Nicely for comments. His family in the USA have confirmed that he and his son, always his father's biggest critic and a "royal pain", have been missing for some time. They could not understand how Jimmy and his son could have become reconciled, therefore they doubted the identifications from India. "JJ was an anarchist, and then a socialist, for God's sake!" The cousin of Nicely snr. spat the words like poison from someone else's snake bite. But the family also confirmed that Nicely had left a "surprisingly small amount" of his enormous fortune to the family, immediately following receipt of insurance compensation for the loss of his church in Colorado.

"The search for the Nicelys continues. Perhaps more importantly, the delivery of necessities to those in need continues. That is the evening news from the BBC tonight. Goodnight."

Leon explained that Nicely appeared to be on the run from "Big Oil", having mis-appropriated almost a trillion dollars before leaving the USA. He repeated, "trillion", "ten to the power of twelve!". The images accompanying the telemetry appeared of mercenaries and secret ops forces scanning regions in the eastern mountains of Afghanistan. Also, the US President had gone all the way to declare Nicely and JJ as "public enemies numbers one, and two, in no particular order."

In stark contrast, banners in a massive street and boat protest in San Francisco declared "Jimmy and JJ for President", and "J&JJ public allies numbers 1 & 2!"

Incredible though this was, Leon then showed us footage of a new music group, called The Nicelies, headed by a sixty-something Irish singer-songwriter by the name of Brendan O'Brien. O'Brien was then apparently three weeks freshly sober. Their "Celtic-Reggae" style was punching out their first hit, "The Benevolent Monks of Bangladesh". The music was really catching, and the group was an overnight success, riding on, and advertising the Nicely gravy train. The United States President's Office offered no comments, when asked by CNN about this new hit.

"Oh my, the cheek of some people..." I chuckled, shaking my head. "But, do you think Nicely's epiphany was because of his son, or an Act of God?" I asked Rosie, in astonishment.

"Maybe his son was the real Act of God," said Rosie, smiling, and laughing, "can you imagine being the parents of Martin Luther King Jnr.?"

"No I can't... but, if Nicely can do something like this, maybe there is hope, for everyone, back home, after all. He could make a believer out of me, I think," I said. It sank in immediately. Then I could not actually believe what I had said, not yet. Maybe I was wrong, but I would suspend that disbelief, for now.

Chapter 17

On tau Ceti 2

"Mom, dad! That was the best, coolest thing I have ever done. The rocket engines were so strong, and noisy. Peter and I just laughed and laughed as it pushed us backwards and forwards in the ship. We never had such fun!"

"Well, except maybe messing around in zero-g!" piped up Peter.

"But there was much more shoving and pushing than boring old Nantucket! And just before we landed with a bump on the ground these other rockets fired and then, well after a while, a whole load of Luna's friends came up and we were all stuck sideways for a bit and I got my hair stuck in the helmet, and..."

"Andrea, sweetie!" said Rosie, very happy and very relieved, "Slow down a moment. We're so glad you are there safely, it must be very exciting. Just tell me where you are and what you are doing." We looked at each other nervously over the video link, we were on separate ships still. "We are interested in what you see and how you feel, both you and Peter, maybe you can describe things as you go along."

"OK mom. So, we landed a pretty good distance from the underground safety area – the colony – that Luna's friends are in. It's very misty outside, a bit windy, it is raining. I don't know if it is warm or cold, our suits keep us comfortable."

"38 Celcius out there, according to the suit telemetry," I said to Rosie, "DC in summertime. No cherry blossoms in that wind though," Rosie did not react to my attempt at humor, which sprang, as usual, from my own nervousness. Maybe she was getting used to it after all.

"We are riding on a kind of tractor/tank thing. There are no roads but a grassy muddy field, and it seems like it might be close to nighttime."

"No Andrea, the sun is up," said Peter, "remember what Luna showed us about our orbit and landing. But it does seem pretty dark. Wow, the wind suddenly got really strong, hold on!" We both looked at each other, concerned. "We're OK, just a really big gust," said Peter, a huge piece of a tree went by not far away."

"We can see lights through the fog- Luna says it is the underground place! I have looked around but I can't see very far, there are no trees or hills or animals, nothing but this underground... No, wait! There is something... a mountain? It's gone. No, there, a very very tall mountain, with sharp tops like, like the photo we saw from Hatteras Light. It's not quite the same as the picture though, and, oh, it's gone again. I never saw such pointed rocks. It's funny, we can't see far along the ground, but sometimes I look up and all the way through this mist or fog, and see the mountains."

Curious, I thought. We would get ground-fogs like this in winter in Maine, but this was a hot climate. I doubted that there was anything in our archive cubes with weather remotely like what the kids were experiencing.

"We have arrived at the entrance. Andrea, Peter, please stay on the vehicle," we could hear Luna, "we will be inside in a moment." I was now holding my breath, watching Peter's visorcam feed, watching my daughter's wide-eyed and awe-struck face as she was to be welcomed by an entirely new and alien race.

"Here we go, I love you mom and dad," said Andrea. I had to swallow hard to stop myself from falling apart. I heard Rosie mutter,

"Oh God," under her breath, and then, louder, "we love you too honey, we are with you the whole way." The door rose painfully slowly, from the ground up, revealing a flood of bright light, rays of white light intermingled with dark stripes radiated all around in the mist. The vehicle moved in. We could see nothing at all, initially. Only after the visorcams adjusted to the new light level and we saw our first view of the interior of the colony, did I realize I was standing rigid, fists and jaw clenched, shoulders hunched. I forced myself to relax, and breathe again.

"Jeez dad, take it easy," said Colin from my shoulder, "they're having fun, after all. Wish I were there too." I laughed, nervously. We watched as all three astronauts were greeted by one heavily be-suited person, who gently guided them, as agreed, to a sealed living area for rest, testing, de-contamination and observation. So far so good, and the kids knew exactly the routine. After one Earth day they would be declared fit or unfit to meet their new friends face to face. I did not want to anticipate the latter.

The suited-up person took some initial medical samples once helmets and suits were removed. Andrea, Peter and Luna were all subject to identical treatment, after all, Luna was no longer just exposed to Cetacean biology. After all, she was as "contaminated" as the alien children themselves.

"Mom, dad, I think I'm really going to like these people, especially if they are all like Luna." said Andrea. "The small man who helped us get undressed kept smiling and being very nice to us, even though we were all in our suits. He seemed very friendly."

"I hope they are like Luna too, and I feel sure you will like them and they will like you. You will be like super-stars there, like royalty, the first of our kind that any of them have ever met."

"How are we supposed to act?" asked Peter, a little worried.

"You're not supposed to act at all." said Wendy, "Just be yourselves. You represent the best that humanity can offer, just by being yourselves. You have done something no-one has ever done. You have landed on an alien planet, using an alien ship, and are being welcomed by an alien civilization. Books will be written about Christopher Columbus, Neil Armstrong, Andrea Kerr and Peter Cowling, all in the same sentence."

"Cool..." Two children's voices came over the audio.

Rosie chimed in. "I know you're both probably very excited, but you will be in isolation for some time until the real meeting takes place. So, would you like to be left alone now for a while? We can let you rest, there is not much you or we can do right now. We are excited to hear how the colony receives you, later."

"I guess so", said Andrea somewhat reluctantly. "I guess I am a *bit* tired." They had been awake over 20 hours. "I could take a nap, I suppose."

"I think that's a great idea. Luna said they would keep the air pressure near normal for us, gradually decreasing to their levels over a couple of days. Just think how refreshed you will be when you meet Luna's friends. Have a good rest, and give us a call if you ever need to talk," Wendy finished.

We watched as Luna gathered the two young children together on a lounger-come-bed. The three snuggled together. The last thing we heard before closing the communicators was

"Luna, can you tell us a story?"

"I will, if you will tell one to me, first" said Luna.

"OK," said Andrea. I wondered if Luna did not know how to tell a story, but she was about to find out firsthand.

The video feed went blank, leaving four of us adults all looking at tired, pale images of one another. We looked drained, but a little relieved. We chatted for a few minutes about how we felt. In the end we all decided the kids were in excellent shape, and that we should try to rest. Our sleep cycles had been ignored, and we knew we ran risks of making mistakes, and short tempers would cause problems too.

In bed alone, I could again not sleep, as was now, apparently, my habit. I decided to think at least one thing through properly. Through my adult life I had found that thinking through a particular physics or astronomy problem, I would get back to a place of comfort, familiarity. More often than not, this would help me fall asleep. So I began.

Would it have been better if the adults had been able to go to the surface, should we have tried hard to make that happen? I felt sure the kids would be treated well, but would they get sick? How would they cope with a different species, the much lower air pressure, the new flora and fauna, bacteria? The list seemed almost infinite. Would they want their parents? This was not the good, comfortable start to a good night's sleep I had hoped for. So I decided to try to think more abstractly, less personally.

Children. Adults. Innocence. Experience. Hope. Despair. Skepticism. Words, simple and complicated. Which word would I choose to describe a children's delegation to, well, anywhere? To me, 'unadulterated' is an unattractive, no, downright ugly-sounding word. Maybe it is not even an acceptable word to some, being a negative-noun-made-into-adjective or some such thing. But it does describe better than any other what the Cetaceans would see in these kids. They would not see an unattractive, pessimistic, officious, aggressive or ugly side of humanity. They would see honesty, innocence, perhaps some vulnerability. But the children would radiate hope. What better thing could humanity offer? It was still a genuine hope, albeit yet without shape or form. That would come, in time. I smiled remembering Rosie's advice: one step at a time.

As my mind began to withdraw along an imaginary warm, misty, meandering river under our own setting Sun, I gratefully held on to the realization that this simple fact is all that was important. After traveling twelve light years, our kids were taking one thing at a time, and we would watch, listen, and follow when we could. Through a mere twist of fate, they could fit inside the de-orbiting ships. So they were the vanguard, the leaders. We were the followers. This was not only right, but it was good, much more than good enough for the here and now. I wondered if it would be possible for the people back on Earth to welcome a children's delegation from Cetacea, one day... That was my last conscious thought in a very long day.

Chapter 18

Exchange

A day or so later, the time came for contact between species. Full communication links were established between the Nantucket, the station, and the colony. Luna, Andrea and Peter had been thoroughly screened, and after a short de-contamination procedure, they were to be welcomed by the entire known population of the entire planet. We were all relieved that this next step had gone so smoothly. They stepped out of the confinement chamber and into the native atmosphere of Cetacea itself. We watched nervously, anticipating irrationally that one of the children might choke and drop to the ground. But all was well.

We heard Peter say excitedly "This is the first fresh air I can remember breathing. It seems 'soft', 'fragrant', it seems friendly. I love breathing it! I am going to like this place! And I can jump again!" We could hear Luna translate in the background as Peter leapt up and down in excitement, a huge grin on his face. The crowd of sixty immediately erupted into a cheer, smiles everywhere.

"Peter is a hit, a natural diplomat," said Rosie to Wendy. Hearing this over the comm link, Ian smiled at me, and Barrie looked very pleased with her twin brother.

With a simple, "This is our people's gift to your people", Andrea handed our gift of the "Encyclopedia Terra" cube to one of the colonists, who looked in astonishment. It was accepted and treated with extreme care. Andrea received the equivalent device, presumably "Encyclopedia Cetacea" graciously, with a classical curtsy.

"Oh my!" came over the audio link, it was Rosie. I too was impressed with her ballet-style flourish. The crowd reacted with obvious pleasure, and perhaps not a little surprise. This was, apparently, a Cetacean move, which she had presumably learned from Luna.

Now Ian had stashed yet another bottle from Earth, from France, in fact. A half bottle of Dom Perignon appeared. He was on the verge of popping the cork, when Colin shouted

"Wait! Ian, wait! That's not a good idea- how are you going to get that stuff into something we can drink out of?"

Like a magician, Ian produced a funny-looking thick-ish plastic bag out of his pocket, "Ta-dah! I planned this out ten years ago! First official meeting between civilizations and no champagne? Come on, guys." He had an ingenious way of getting champagne into the bag, along with the cork. We then took turns sipping from the bag, Colin and even Barrie having sips. To make bubbles "rise" Colin whizzed the bag around his head. Wendy and Rosie were quite jealous. "I have one for you too, but you'll have to come and get it!"

Afterwards Ian, Colin and I had a good laugh at Ian's craftiness. "So what is that bag thing anyway, Ian? Something medical perhaps?" I was trying to be funny. Ian looked a trifle embarrassed.

"Errm, well, you'd probably better not pursue that line of inquiry any further," he said.

"What do you mean dad?" asked Colin.

"It doesn't matter Colin, clean plastic bags have a lot of medical uses." I was pretty sure this was something usually not used to get stuff *into* the body.

After these celebrations, we had to settle down to the business of working together with the Cetaceans. On precisely what, we did not yet know, but we started with communication, naturally. From orbit, Luna had instructed her engineers to make a simple interface, including some software written for our 64 bit information encoding. A team of 15 individuals in the colony were assigned to work with the cube. Five more were to work with Luna to develop software to translate English into Cetacean, both written and spoken forms. No more could be spared from those doing the jobs essential to maintaining the colony.

Luna had pointedly asked that, while in isolation, she and the children should be left to do what they wanted. She needed them to feel at home with someone they knew and trusted. In conversations with Rosie, we adults became struck by Luna's uncanny ability to see so clearly what the children might need. It seemed that perhaps not just the biology was convergent, but that even emotional needs may be too. Luna was certainly no child, in spite of her very child-like appearance. Perhaps we were witnessing the beginnings of an entirely new academic, even clinical, subject for study: "convergent psychology". Maybe this would eventually carry more importance even than than the famous identical twin "nature versus nurture" investigations and debates. Rosie had joked, when we first discovered the alien signals, that she could always get a future job in alien-human clinical psychology. Sometimes life has a way of taking our jokes seriously. I would have to watch for that myself in future.

As soon as Luna was released from isolation, she began introductions using her talent in rapid mental communications. She projected episodes of our lunar encounters for the Cetaceans, introducing the other six of us and summarized her interpretation of our roles and skills. After this she communicated clearly in words, succinctly, our mission to tau Ceti 2. All of this took her a mere ten minutes, from beginning to end.

At this point Andrea and Peter were introduced in some depth. From our vantage point in orbit we were astonished to hear both Peter and Andrea communicate briefly in the Cetacean language. The locals were again delighted with the children's early attempts to engage with them on their terms. Luna looked proud. The limits of their communication skills were soon reached though, and they were asked to join a group for refreshments, and what appeared to be a movie. It was the beginning of their new education. At this point, we signed off, it was an intense couple of hours.

Even with all the positive feelings I had about Luna, I still felt nervous. We simply had to trust these new alien people. We had to believe in them. *Credo*: I believe; I have faith. This faith became a little easier knowing that the children had apparently become physically acclimatized to their new surrounds. They did look very healthy, a very good color, even under the artificial lights of the colonial underground sanctuary.

In the meantime, the fifteen engineers had already completed the first part of their work, they had gotten their own interface to work with the Encyclopedia Terra cube. More than this, they had worked in reverse as well, so that we could now begin read their hardware. All that was needed was for Luna to provide the user interface that was translated into English for us. Over on the station, Rosie and Wendy had been instructed in the philosophy behind the use of the station's computer system, but it was not until an upload from the ground that the new, still crude interface could be used to explore the banks of data. "Nantucket, do you copy?" asked Rosie.

"We copy." said Colin, overlooked by Ian while Barrie and I were preparing dinner. "What can we do for you mom?"

"Hi honey, we are going to up-link a large amount of data to Nantucket, stand by." Colin monitored the data transfer, it would take 40 hours or so to complete using microwaves, but no-one was planning on going anywhere until we were all safely on our ship. "These data are the Encyclopedia Cetacea, or at least that is what we call it. It is equivalent to our own world history, so far as we can tell. We have been looking at images of the planet through history here, at the moment we have no way to read or understand any language. The surface teams will provide crude translation software, with Luna's help, as soon as a day from now. They appear to be very talented, they have already achieved this much very quickly. I guess we will find out soon enough."

"Roger that mom, I see some data already. I shall fiddle myself with a few things, to see if I can figure out some stuff. This is going to be fun."

"Hey Colin," said Wendy from the station, "you can look for yourself in these data, the history continues to be written into this database, the Nantucket is one of the latest, and probably most important entries."

"Cool!" said Colin. "I wonder what I'll find, I wonder what they think of us..."

Barrie had been listening while cooking. She said, with a big smile, "I guess we are part of history, huh?"

"On two planets. Not many people can say that!" I said.

"Eight. Just eight people." said Barrie, still smiling, and preparing her own form of muesli. "I'm going to help Colin figure out some stuff, some difficult stuff."

Chapter 19

Knowledge

Within two more days we received the first working interfaces and translation software from the colony. Ian and I looked over it and were astonished at the quality of the work. Translations were spec'ed as accurate to better than a 0.1%, but we felt it was much better than that. The Cetacean software was evidently far in advance of anything we had seen. The more the machines learned, the more accurate their algorithms became. The software was self-adapting, re-writing itself to optimize the tasks it was given. It got faster and faster, the more it was used. The Cetaceans had somehow solved problems that had so hindered logicians and engineers on Earth, right when they always appeared on the verge of computational breakthroughs. "I would love to look into their solutions of the classic conundrums and theorems that faced our mathematicians and logicians back home," said Ian.

"Well, with your pedigree, your decoding of the first Cetacean signals behind you, you would be the right guy to take a look." I said.

"Don't tell him that! He's vain enough as it is!" came Wendy's voice over the comms link. Ian only smiled, and shook his head. "You know I'm just pulling your leg, right honey?" came Wendy's voice. "I agree with Michael, I could not think of anyone better! Go for it!"

It had been decided that, pending another suitable break in the cyclonic weather, a small delegation was to arrive at the station from the ground in order to help us navigate the history of an entire planet. Ian had requested to see some of the algorithms in their computer code, and was assured that a member of the delegation was looking forward to working with him.

We in Nantucket would stay and take part from our few km distant orbital station. Rosie and Wendy were to receive the group and work with them. We had collectively all agreed that we should start from the status quo and, in our quest to move forward, look at the two histories of our planets. We would start from the current situation and work backwards as needed. But first we were given a crash course in some of the defining moments in Cetacean history, culture and philosophy, to try to give us a foundation upon which we could build understanding.

The knowledge we acquired was at the same time fascinating and heartbreaking. The Cetaceans emerged relatively recently from millennia of trial-and-error engineering, agriculture, construction, seafaring. There were strong parallels with humanity's achievements prior to our industrial development. In their modern age, the laws of nature were systematically uncovered, understood and put to the good of much of society. Beasts of burden were replaced with machines. Machines succeeded and populations grew vastly in temperate regions of the planet. More machines, more people. More people, more machines. People needed food and water. Machines needed energy.

Some three hundred Earth-years ago, nuclear energy had begun to be produced, fissile material being discovered in various pockets planet-wide. The success of the nuclear program produced a century long stable era of almost free energy. Radioactive by-products were a serious issue, the Cetacean's early solution had been to bury material deep. Later, when their chemically powered rockets became essentially failure-free, they launched the material into deep space, never to return. The nuclear fusion programs were looking promising, but those "clean" reactors always seemed to be "just 10 orbits into the future".

During the 101st year, two unrelated "accidents" changed the course of the Cetaceans' future. The northern hemisphere of the planet was poisoned by the catastrophic failure of a reactor. Prevailing global winds transmitted lethal radioactive by-products to over a billion souls. Water supplies were poisoned, fish, agriculture, all were poisoned. In ten years a large part of the planet was laid bare. A full strip of latitudes became uninhabitable. A fundamental design flaw common to almost all working reactors was found. After widespread panic a massive team was charged with fixing, once and for all, the problem. But their efforts never got started. The bulk of the southern hemisphere suffered its own nuclear tragedy with almost theatrically melodramatic timing. During a routine launch of a nuclear dustbin rocket, the first stage attitude control was lost as it detached from the second, the rocket and payload were a total loss. The Southern atmosphere was poisoned extensively. It was the first rocket failure in over five decades, and the first carrying a nuclear payload. For significant fractions of the population, the only choice was starvation as ecosystems failed. The lucky ones who could eat, were faced with various levels of radiation poisoning.

Within one generation the population of mammals on the planet had been reduced two-fold. Malignancies were responsible for only a small proportion of the losses worldwide. Political boundaries changed, wars began as fights for water and other necessities began, and billions of refugees fought for survival. These unavoidable political upheavals were to decimate the rest. The need for energy was desperate, power had to be provided, and the only acceptable and tractable way to do this was to burn. Fossil fuel reserves, previously seen by the Cetaceans as energy only for use by ancestors in pre-history, were re-opened, their energy extraction being made possible through a planetary-wide emergency strategy including the development of special hardware, a process supervised by leaders of wealthy nations. But then crops failed as natural weather patterns changed with unfortunate timing, and the machinery could not catch up with demand. Disease spread, water and grain wars began, and expanded. The desperate rush to reinstate the power-dependent society became an heroic struggle, a fight to ban the nuclear option for eternity and to reinstate stability. But they were fighting against hopeless odds. The population at its height was readily supported by their nuclear infrastructure. But it would take years to go from essentially zero power to a level of bare sustenance even for half of the population. The Cetacean population had said clearly, no more nuclear power. The leaders accepted this, knowing the dire consequences for at least half of their citizens. They had decided that they had no other choice.

The Cetacean biosphere was balanced, like the Earth's, in the respiration of oxygen and carbon-dioxide breathing organisms. Unlike Earth though, CO_2 breathers were fewer and less efficient, and so there was more room for CO_2 to increase, a lot more.

The tragedy of Cetacea was excruciatingly difficult for us to hear. The garbage of the nuclear generations poisoned the world for the children and grand-children of the nuclear age. But this garbage, although sometimes fatal, still left a large fraction of Cetacean families unharmed. There were, after all, entire latitude zones left almost untouched by the dispersed radioactive material. The real damage was done by weak leaders of these children and grandchildren. They were unable to resist persuasive business people who had stepped into the energy void as proponents of fossil fuel consumption. These entrepreneurs persuaded essentially everyone that society needed to consume energy in the way that their ancestors had been accustomed to, by burning. It was an easy sell. Detractors were ridiculed, reviled for their lack of vision for the future. The obvious chaos of those years proved without doubt to many that the Cetacean society must get their machines going again. "The machines would feed, protect, keep society warm, bring water, enable business. They would even help to make us happy again, after all we had been through."

And so vast numbers of fossil-fueled power stations were rushed into operation. The machines were fed with energy. The energy worked on food production, water purity, the huge but depleted population was slowly provided for once more. All was well with Cetacea, or would be. Fossil fuel entrepreneurs were rewarded with positions of high authority, were hailed as saviors.

Within three generations, CO_2 levels on the planet doubled. It happened just slowly enough that almost no-one noticed. The people were concerned with political stability, financial security, after their basic needs were met by the new found energy, and after their terrifying global disasters.

Tragically, those generations unknowingly exchanged one kind of instability for another. The Cetacean histories put it like this: While the political leaders were quick to act, most with approval of the desperate populations of frightened people, the planet itself did not have a "fast acting" option to call upon. The planet's trajectory was changed once global-scale combustion started. The planet followed nature's laws, not those desired by society. The atmosphere evolved oh so slowly, the oceans warmed, the ice melted, it went almost unnoticed by the fast-acting leadership. It was understandable, after all they had more urgent matters needing attention.

It was all horribly familiar to us.

"Not that it matters, but I have a question that refuses to go away," said Rosie after we had taken a break from our historical, sociological studies. "Would you rather end up with a changed climate through ignorance, for whatever reason, or by denial?"

"You don't seriously expect me to answer that, do you?" I replied. I could feel tension building again in my tightening jaw. "Those poor Cetaceans, though, just how tragic is their recent history?"

"You don't seriously expect me to answer *that*, do you?" replied Rosie. "But I do know what you mean, it is a terrifying tragedy. Sixty-two. Just sixty-two left. God Almighty."

"I don't know what he, or she, has to do with it." I said.

"Yes, religion with a capital "R" never was your strong-point," said Rosie with a weak smile, resignedly.

Chapter 20

Options

Just five days after Andrea and Peter had reached the surface, they reported that they thought they had taught the Cetaceans about as much as they could that might be immediately useful. They would be able to study our cube data themselves, from now on. Peter had introduced them to Dr. Who as if it were historical, but his fun was spoiled when some of the early cyber-men produced great laughter. Peter had to explain that while it was "low-budget", the use of egg-cartons and dish-soap containers on their costumes was pretty creative, and part of its "charm". He had a very difficult time trying to explain this concept, but he did not shy from trying. After a clarification by Luna, the laughter became an uproar, and Peter, while a bit confused and upset, could not help but join in. We all needed some humor. Earlier, Colin and I had indulged a bit on the Nantucket with some ancient Laurel and Hardy. That was almost childish enough for me.

One of the three Cetaceans aboard the neighboring station came on the screen and said, in the smooth tones of Silky English, "We would like all of us to discuss and decide on where we might go from here. We believe that our exchange of factual knowledge is sufficient for us to begin a meaningful symposium. Perhaps we can now rest and convene in 12 Earth hours?"

"Rosie and I suggested this" said Wendy, "we would do it over the videocomm as usual. I am getting tired of being over here and Peter being down there, I think the sooner we can establish some kind of plan, the better."

"What about me? Don't you miss me?" asked Ian.

"Oh, you know what I meant, I'm 'here' not 'there' with you and Barrie. Of course I miss you."

"Now now," I interrupted, "we're all tired and miss one another. But yes, we agree," Ian nodded. "Twelve hours it is then. It will be wonderful to look a little further down the road, and begin to tread the path of opportunity. Goodnight."

"My, we are feeling poetic tonight!" Ian said.

"I'm trying to be optimistic, to be humanistic, to be... oh never mind! You won't understand, you're a damned mathematician." Ian laughed out loud at that one.

Colin and I had now got almost half way through Robinson Crusoe, and he read another chapter to me. He yawned, said "I think that is it for me tonight," turned over and was soon sleeping. I turned over, and slept.

The next thing I was aware of was a familiar and enticing smell. Colin came in with coffee in the baby-sippy-cup. I thought it was about 30 seconds after I fell asleep. Boy, was I still that tired? This was going to be a hard day. He left, I "staggered around" weightlessly. I thought perhaps the endless weeks of sleep problems had come home to roost. I was vaguely aware of hearing a musical conversation. Cetacean. After some more maneuvers in bathroom and sink, and dressing, I made my way to the large cabin to find Colin conversing nicely with a Cetacean on-screen. I had never noticed much language skill in his classes, but this was different. "Thanks for the coffee Colin," I yawned, "how come you are speaking their language so well?"

"Oh, this is Sha-sha, she has been teaching me and I have been studying." He continued with his aria. Hmm. I wonder what he has been studying, precisely, I thought. This could be very tricky, it's wonderful to have feelings, but we are a species that survives through the mandate of sexual reproduction, that is a hard urge to suppress, if indeed it should be suppressed at all. I was snapped back to the present, thankfully, with Colin's keen voice,

"Dad, she wants to know what an astronomer does."

"Er, well, it's been a while, can I explain later?"

"OK." Colin then signed off and came over for breakfast.

"I got really good at learning the language with the translator, I can read a bit too."

"That is really impressive." It was good to see my teenager get really interested in something.

"Well, we'll see. I have a feeling there are a lot of nuances that we miss, they think differently from us," he said. He then explained some more observations of the language, in some detail, but it washed over my head as it throbbed and it was all I could do to keep eyes open, and remain conscious. I did notice though that he was showing considerable signs of maturity, he was making great strides towards becoming an adult. Eventually he finished with a short sentence, the first I had noted for a minute or so. "So what do you think dad?"

"What? Err, sure. Fine. What time is..?"

"Really? I can? That's great!" I decided not to quiz him more, I needed a shower, some pain killers, more sleep, or something. So I returned to the bathroom.

An hour later our meeting, or "symposium" as Silky had translated it, began. The agenda had been sent earlier. There was one item. "Options". This might be a very short or very long meeting. I could not tell. But it did seem to me that our options had increased since we arrived in our planetary orbit. I stopped and tried to appreciate what that meant. Yes, we really did have options.

Then, on the videocomm link came a list

1. Nantucket and entire crew return to Earth.

2. Nantucket, some crew and some Cetaceans go to Earth.

3. Nantucket and crew stay with Cetaceans.

"This list was decided and compiled by Andrea and Peter, along with all of us on the ground. Please, let us discuss possible benefits," said the translated voice of Luna. Option 2. shocked me, I was not mentally ready for splitting our crew, or even considering such a thing. I had not expected to discuss departures, I had wondered about more mundane things, such as getting water to Nantucket. I could see surprise on the faces of Rosie and Wendy on the monitor.

This list was simple. It was either too simple or brilliantly clear.

Then I saw the way forward. There was only one possible option.

"Dad, what is it, dad?" asked Colin, responding to some expression on my face. Ian and Barrie looked in my direction too. "Let's listen to the discussion, shall we?" I said.

Chapter 21

Wisdom

Luna led the meeting, we were all using the translation software. "I am authorized to speak on behalf of our people. We have shared the total knowledge of our civilizations, of which we have studied only a tiny fraction. But knowledge is only a pre-requisite for what we really need, and that is *wisdom*.

"What we know now about humanity, from Andrea and Peter, is that you think and care and feel in similar ways to us. While there are differences, some big, we are nevertheless alike, and we have found that we like each other. As Cetaceans, we feel that we should help one another. Our interstellar call for help was successful, against all odds. We did not expect it to work. When your responses arrived we hoped that we might learn from you, in spite of problems on Earth that we could see, but not yet understand. When we knew that Nantucket had landed on our moon, our people's outlook changed, we were euphoric. You offered us hope, for surely your technology was far in advance of ours, or so we thought. But since then we have learned of Earth's desperate problems and the nature of your mission here. We met to discuss your, and our, situations, for two days. It was for us, a difficult time. But we eventually were able to appreciate your first words to us. We believed we were better off with you here, than without you. We would learn from one another, and move forwards.

"That is our position. So, our task here and now has become very clear. We, the 62 of us and 8 of you, must consider the futures of *two* entire civilizations. One is at the very brink of extinction, another on the same trajectory. One is no more or less important than the other. Both are in terrible danger. Both have caused new and different climate conditions, both must live with consequences for several generations. That is our shared reality.

"There is no 'quick fix' for these problems. No amount of planetary resources can be used, no political, industrial, scientific solutions exist to enable any of us to live as our predecessors did, even if we wanted to. There is surely a slower solution, yet this cannot be a solution for us to achieve in our lifetimes. Instead it is a solution for our grandchildren, and their grandchildren. For the living Cetacean people, this is solution enough. It is enough to know we will secure a planet for our offspring, to pass along a world better than the one we were given.

"So our plan here is to continue with absolutely minimal combustion. We will try to find those new and fertile areas. We will try to help vegetation and trees grow in new micro-climate zones, through trans-plantation, and to rebuild animal stocks. In the meantime, we must wait for our global CO_2 levels to drop. We believe that they will drop as the biological carbon sinks begin to flourish and grow in abundance with the excess CO_2. We are developing plant forms using cross-fertilization to optimize carbon sequestration, in our cloud-enshrouded world. We will also try to re-seed our oceans with algae and cyanobacteria that we know should survive best in our changed climate. We will study your Earth-based research to see if there is something more we can do to aid these efforts. We are a tiny colony, and we now burn no carbon fuel. Energy from wind and water suffices for our colony. So our job here is one of patience, and of having children, many children. Eventually we may find other survivors, our job is also to seek them out.

"In short, our survival strategies, our tasks on this planet are simple to state. For some of us it will be difficult to live only for the future generations. But in truth, it is the Earth that faces the severest difficulties. The cruelest eras are mostly in our past. You will face the decades of tempests and raging winds and seas that have taken almost all of our people, one way or another. You will continue to face deniers, and their powerful political allies. For it will not be among the poor and disenfranchised where you find the deniers. They never had anything to lose from their first instant on Earth."

Luna stopped, abruptly. We sat in a dark mood, in a respectful and grim silence, following this all-too-accurately painted picture of our situation. The Cetacean's stark words had left such a weight of gravity in the air, things of such significance, I could barely lift my head even to begin to think of a place to start, even if I wanted to. These difficulties had dragged me down into the deep and heavy turbulence, buried at the back of in my mind. In this state of mind I felt stifled, unable to see a way though. There were too many things to deal with, not least of which was our separation in time from the Earth. The worst of these moments made me panic, I always felt like I struggled to get enough air. I felt I was trying to breath a dank, heavy, polluted mist. In my darkest moments, I was living in the deepest parts of a dirty, violent river, an environment so dark, so heavy, it would steal all light, it would banish all air, and life, and force me down to oblivion.

Andrea's voice came gently through this stifling atmosphere. "Uh, mom, dad, everyone. I have been thinking, as well as learning while I have been here. I think our choice is really pretty simple. If Nantucket returns with all of us then we have all the Cetacean's knowledge, but none of their wisdom goes with us. You see, I don't know what wisdom is, really, but I do know it is alive and inside someone, some people, maybe even most people. A book can sometimes have wisdom in it, but wisdom, really useful wisdom, is alive, it's part of living people, it's part of Luna, I know it is.

"So, if we stay here, all of us, we can transmit some of their wisdom home, they could use the translator to talk to Bishop Rock right now, but each side of a conversation would take 12 years. That's no good either! I think instead, that to get some of their wisdom to Earth, to help the people there before the Earth boils over, then there has to be a Cetacean, 'there and then', down on Earth. Well, that's what I think, anyway."

Perhaps one or two of the turbulent eddies pulling at my thoughts had been lightened by these words of my sweet, young daughter, young, but apparently wise already. The air around me felt just a little bit easier to breathe. I wondered how the others might respond.

"By God, I think..., I believe she's got it." whispered Ian. "The answer, and wisdom too!" He spoke loudly.

"Andrea, what can I say? You spoke for us all here, and I think you may be right. You see things so clearly."

"What do you, Michael, Rosie, Ian, Wendy, think of Andrea's suggestion?" Silky translated from Luna.

"Well, errm, we will need to discuss this further..." I started.

"You should know that all colonists agree with Andrea's position, she told us about this yesterday, and we have had time to digest." This time, Luna replied in English itself, not Silky English.

"Wow, well, OK then. Errm, we'll still have to discuss this. I think we should have some time for digestion too. We'll get back to you as soon as we can. I hope that is satisfactory."

"Thank you, we will stand by. Let us know when we can help. We will let the humans here have some private time, we Cetaceans will retire and rest now. Over and out."

"What are we going to do now?" I heard Rosie say a minute later over the comm link. I had asked the same question of Rosie when first faced with the possibility of interstellar flight. In spite of my earlier depressive state, I could not help but permit myself a small chuckle. Was Andrea only fifteen? Yes, so far as I was able to count properly.

Chapter 22

Decision

"Well, these Cetacean guys don't mess around!" I said, "I mean, what happened to all the red tape and politicians and opinions and..." I stopped. I could tell that my attempt at levity was misplaced. The actual answer to my question was so awful, I felt ashamed, so I continued instead with "I'm sorry everyone, I don't know what I was thinking, I was trying to be funny. There are only sixty-two of them, of course."

"Well, we appreciate the attempt, but OMG!" said Rosie. "How old are you anyway?" I apologized again and thought, "too old, yet obviously not old enough!" Rosie did have the decency to laugh at that attempt.

"I like the way they do things," interjected Ian, "I think we should try to see things as straight-forwardly as possible. I suggest we start by looking at the recommended option. Simplicity does not mean childish naïveté, in fact..."

"Well you were selected for this mission because of your 'simple' decryption of the original message. You are bound to like the way they do things!" said Wendy. I was impressed at how clearly everyone seemed to be thinking today.

"OK, OK," Ian said, "but they have given us a way forward. Any objections to talking *first* about option 2? No? Good!"

We separated our discussion into the potential needs of humanity, and our own needs. Regarding the first, we talked about many points. There was no guarantee that Cetaceans would be able to help humanity, other than that option 2. seemed a very good bet. Indeed, face-to-face meetings were the reason we left on our journey eight years before.

On a return journey, we could all use the time to do significant research, and could discuss options for Earth's future upon our return. At the same time we would witness effects of terrestrial global warming, accelerated in time by our rapidly decreasing distance to Earth. With humans and Cetaceans working together on Nantucket, we believed our chances of finding solutions to Earth's political problems might be higher. Behind all these thoughts though was the knowledge that the only solution to Earth's problems would be the patient sacrifices made by several generations.

We also considered the psychological impact of arriving on Earth with two, or maybe four, Cetaceans. Our mission was predicated on the idea that actual physical contact was going to be paramount. But no-one had anticipated that the nature of this first contact would be so physically and literally critical for survival and for generating mutual trust. So, to arrive on Earth *without* Cetaceans would place the rest of humanity a critical step further from accepting them, their advice, experience, knowledge and wisdom. In short, the peoples of Earth needed to touch, feel, hear and see for themselves. Unlike the other options, purely for humanity's sake, we saw no down-sides to option 2.

Our discussion reluctantly passed to the question of who would stay, who would go. We asked Luna the simple question. "How many Cetaceans should go." The answer came quickly, from the male called Shay-Shay.

"Four. We must send Luna and two other pregnant females, and one male Cetacean. We have genetic seed and eggs that must be sent as well for maximal genetic diversity of those of our race living on Earth. The offspring of our selected individuals are known to include 3 females and a male twin, carried by Luna. For us it is a question of simple genetic diversity, and females to carry and nurture offspring. The unrelated male is needed to represent our gender diversity to people of Earth, and he is needed as an addition of genetic diversity for a second colony on Earth."

So this was the hand we were dealt. We could not deny the logic, we could not deny the Cetacean's insurance policy of a new life, on Earth. There was no way we could think of to reduce the number of our fellow travelers to 3, and two was out of the question. Four it had to be.

Four of us would stay with the Colony. The children played the deciding cards for us, it was a terrible decision for us to make, heart-breaking. It simply had to be a family group, we all agreed that there was nothing to gain from splitting parents, children, spouses. So, it was a question of seeing if there were one family better suited to a give choice than another. Colin began the discussion.

"Dad, you said I could stay here if I wanted."

"I did what? I did no such thing young man!" I recalled my thoughts about Colin's approaching manhood.

"Yes you did, here, just a few days ago. You remember? Please say you remember..."

I recalled agreeing to something when I was so tired. Oh no, surely not that. I could not imagine it would be this! "Oh but Colin, I did not sleep the previous night, and I was not able to think properly at all, I just wanted a little space then for later discussions."

"I knew that, dad. I am smarter than you think. But I like these people, you know? I really *like* them, I think I would be as happy here as I could be at home after another eight years of travel or so. I have thought about this, there is something about these people..."

"But Colin, you have no idea what you are suggesting here, I mean, you are a teen, you have traveled in isolation with just two families, and you do still have relatives at home, and.." interrupted Rosie.

"But mom, I am not a kid. I have emotional needs, and at least one of the Cetaceans seems to understand me better than, well, better than any human has! Honestly."

"OK Colin, we hear you clearly," said Rosie, "I know I am your mom but remember also I am a psychologist. I do acknowledge what you're saying, and I will not underestimate it. But let's hear from others too. That will help."

Ian explained that he was wondering how he could go back to Earth and face such a complex situation, and travel for many years again. "The only way I could do it is with Wendy, Peter and Barrie, if we were to go, I would I think be able to cope."

"Does that mean you'd rather stay?" Asked Wendy.

"No, I could stay here but it would have to be with my family. That is what is most important, honestly."

I said, "I feel pretty much the same."

Rosie began, "Ian, I think that none of us is thinking of leaving our family, that would be a bad idea. We simply need to decide which family will stay. For that family it almost certainly means never setting foot on Earth again, at least for the parents. Let's be completely clear on that at least.

"Is that true?" asked Colin, "You see the Cetaceans have blueprints for Nantucket and all the data from our flight. I reckon they could build a new, even better one, in a few years."

"He's right" said Ian, in optimistic tones.

"Very good," said Rosie, "let's see what other individuals think. So far, I think we can say we have a preference from Colin," I shook my head, "err, hmm. As I said a preference from Colin, and a no-preference from Ian. So far, so good. Let's hear from the rest of the children first."

Peter explained that, not remembering anything of Earth, his only family was the seven of us until some days ago. When he emerged from isolation on the planet, he became captivated by his new friends, and his family had grown from 7 to 70. He spoke of several Cetaceans as "uncles", "aunts", friends, he rattled off a few un-pronounceable names, and said he would be sad to leave them. But if some came along for the ride with him to Earth, that would be good too. Barrie really like Luna and wanted to be with her, but her main concern was leaving her family, and that she would be really sad if she were not to see Wendy, Colin, Andrea and me any more.

Andrea had fallen in love with friends on the planet, she was almost fluent in the language already, knew several word games, played a musical instrument like an oboe, and was learning to cook. Five years of creative energy was being unleashed to the delight of her new friends. She did not even seem to miss Rosie and I, but then her visit had always been understood as a temporary one. When pushed between staying and leaving with Cetaceans, she said both would be OK, provided Luna was one of them that would be with her.

Rosie began, "I confess my preference is very simple, to be with my family. That is all, except that I really do not look forward to another eight years in space, but I could do it."

Wendy replied, "I feel just the same way. I want to add that I would be very interested in working with the Cetaceans on their biology, and clinical practices. I could do this both on the trip home as well as on the planet."

We looked at each other on the screens. "Want to sleep on it?" asked Ian, "or should we try to decide?"

Rosie seemed to be most interested in this entire decision process, and said "How about we try something. It seems that either family would genuinely do fine, staying, or leaving. I believe I would honestly be happy with either option. Closing doors on Earth does sound drastic and painful, but then going back to the pandemonium there also seems very painful. Also I believe whoever stays here will have a useful, happy and satisfying life, fighting a different and wholly alien fight for survival. What I suggest is that we let the kids decide. It is their future more than ours. They are all closer to the Cetaceans than us. Let them thrash it out and come up with a solution."

"That makes me very nervous, it's not fair on the kids," I admitted. "We must have the gender, sex, relationship talk with all the kids, those who stay will have no sexual relations, this is a big deal. But I cannot see a better solution. If they get stuck, we draw straws, throw the dice, yes?"

Rosie carefully explained that, during the flight to tau Ceti, she had taken pains to take aside each child to speak in depth with them gently about the meaning of mutual love and how it differs from maternal or paternal love. This was news to me. Welcome news. She was such a caring person, she would want to help the kids with this difficult information, their transitions towards adulthood. "I believe each child now knows what it means to have strong feelings for another. It will be difficult for all of them, no matter who goes or stays. But that was always going to be the case."

The kids accepted this statement as if Rosie were talking about their writing or math skills, it was no big deal to them. Their lives in space had become almost their whole lives, there were only indistinct memories of Earth for our children, none for Peter and Barrie. For them, the Earth was an invisible object next to one of ten thousand stars supposedly visible in the tau Ceti sky.

After a significant pause, Wendy said "But, oh God, it's going to be terribly hard splitting up our families." We all nodded anxiously, nervously. None of us wanted to say anything, it was too difficult.

"Mommy, you're thinking of it all wrong. Just think of the families we will gain, here, in space, or on Earth!" Said Barrie.

We smiled through the odd tear, and agreed, she was right. After more conversation that nervously avoided the issue, we retired, knowing that Rosie's proposal was a good one.

The next day, and with tears in her eyes, Andrea reported the decision from the planet. Rosie led a conversation, making sure the kids would be able to live with their decision, and we took pains to re-affirm it and share the responsibility. We thanked the kids for their help. It was done. The next steps were being taken, one at a time. I felt for Andrea, but I also felt a huge sense of relief.

Shortly after, the weather permitted a launch from the surface. A water-laden ship began its unmanned ascent to the station, to re-stock Nantucket.

Chapter 23

Preparations

In the end, the decision was straightforward. But for Wendy, Ian, Rosie and I, it was also very difficult. Until this point, I realized I still believed that we might, as a family, return to Earth. This was no longer an option. To try to avoid talking of even thinking about it, naturally we made ourselves very busy. Rosie and Wendy worked very hard on preparing the water transfer hardware, and had copied the entire Encyclopedia Cetacea onto one of our cubes. Both moms were looking forward to seeing the kids again. We had three days to prepare for Nantucket's departure. Ian and I had reviewed the flight plan and checked all subsystems, it took two days to be really sure of the integrity of the ship. We were happy with the motor reconfiguration.

"I'm really going to miss you, Ian, in spite of you being such a 'wise guy'. But of course, I'm going to miss your family a lot more." I said, teasingly.

"Oh that's nice, yeah. I will miss you like, like I would miss a bout of gout."

"'Bout of gout'? Really? Where did you get that one from?" I raised my eyebrows high. After a few moments we burst out laughing, and then slowly realized that we were unlikely to see one another again in the flesh. Ever. We found ourselves embracing. "Seriously though, I am scared," I said, "I am definitely going to miss every one of you. You still make me laugh with your dumb comments. I feel we are making the right decision though, and I see no other way out at this point. Your family is my family, I'll be thinking of you a lot in the future."

"Your family is mine too, it will always be so."

"The downside for you is that you will have to get along with Leon again!", I joked, less than convincingly.

Following a two-hour-long delicate maneuver to the space station, Wendy and Rosie successfully transferred all the water we could take. The Cetacean engineers working with them were competent, and fast.

It hit me, again, that "fast" technology was a major contributor to the fates of Earth and Cetacea. This unwelcome reminder always made me feel uneasy, as if I were making a deal with the Devil. Lucifer always required payment at the appointed hour. Something inside me always rebelled against the quick, fast way of doing things. The periods of massive industrial development felt long to an individual, but these were nothing in the natural history of planets. The global warming crises arose precisely because of this simple fact. And here we were, using Cetacean technology developed over mere days that would enable us to fly to Earth, deliver Cetaceans in person, with implications for generations to come. Fast-ness was not wholly bad. The problem seemed to come when *only* operating with such hastiness.

I tried to see things in terms of hope, belief. I simply had to have faith in these few delicate beings that were now my life. With Rosie's counseling, I could see the difference between the "fast-buck" mentality that has sealed the fates negatively in the long-term, and the need to take small steps towards a long-term goal. I remembered something of Adam Smith's core thesis, that "looking out for number one results in prosperity". How damaging that idea had turned out to be, in the hands of massive corporations, to the Earth's ecosystems.

Out of these confused thoughts, I decided that, given the successes of all our joint endeavors in orbit above the planet, I was comfortable with the apparent swiftness of the Cetacean engineers. Indeed, I hoped that their step-by-step approach to protecting the long term was something that the return mission to Earth would successfully communicate upon their arrival.

"The Nantucket seems to be as ready as she needs to be, there's nothing else left to do," said Ian to everyone and no-one. On the ground, the Cetaceans had refitted a freight capsule to accommodate a family, my family, and some necessities. It was launched with ceremony from the ground launch center, just a few kilometers from the colonial underground village. Six hours later it docked with the station. Rosie and Wendy put their heads through the small docking ring, to a big cheer from Peter and Andrea. Three hours later the ship docked using a recently constructed port to the Nantucket, and we were reunited as one big family.

We had one final day of our flight routine, in orbit around Cetacea. We enjoyed movies of Earth's natural beauty, slow beauty. Tidal surges, aurorae, sunsets, moon-rises, bird migrations, schools of whales, time-lapse photography of seasons. We finished with hot chocolate, and a film showing hoards of animals of the Serengeti, a favorite film we had watched perhaps ten times.

The kids wanted a story at bedtime. "Dad, can you read us the bit where Robinson Crusoe meets man Friday?" Asked Colin. Andrea nodded. I smiled, and said

"Of course, but we'll have to talk about Robinson Crusoe some more, the story is for both kids and adults. You guys are ready to read a bit more deeply. For now we will pretend we are all kids, and just enjoy the story." If only I could do that more, I thought. But that was a naïve thought in itself. Once that innocence was gone, it was not possible to read some of the best books the same way again. It was not possible to "un-read" the darker sides of writings.

"Dad, we know about that, we're not *little* kids anymore," said Colin

"Yeah!" said Andrea. "And tomorrow we will step down onto our own desert island. You and mom are going to love it, but I'm going to miss Luna a lot. She's my best friend in the whole world." In Andrea's world, in her time, in her space, I thought. This world was going to separate from Luna's very soon. I hoped Andrea had made some really good friends on the surface, she was going to need them.

Chapter 24

Parting

Luna and her fellow friends arrived at the Nantucket in the modified ship. The two other females and single male inspected the cabin, and Wendy introduced herself and Barrie and Ian. Peter was so excited, he launched himself uncontrolledly into these new arrivals. He was happily trying out his newly learned language, by apologizing over-elaborately. After this initial mayhem, they selected their berths for the next eight years, and unloaded personal belongings. Luna's memorabilia included a photograph of Andrea. Then the Cetaceans presented our family with personal things with which to remember them. They had prepared recordings of themselves and their families, their histories. Luna seemed especially proud to present hers to Rosie, who became tearful. "Thank you for saving me and my children-to-be-born" she added, "when she is born she will be Rosie, when he is born, he will be Michael."

Rosie and I were struck dumb. "Oh mommy," said Andrea, "that's wonderful!" A tiny Rosie and Michael, would be born on Nantucket, somewhere along the line between Earth and tau Ceti. They would walk on the Earth. The Earth would be their home.

"That's kinda weird." said Colin. Then a large smile showed he was not serious. All we could do was move forward and give Luna a huge hug.

"Luna, you are so kind. This is a real gift to Michael and myself. I wish I could be there for the births, but Wendy will be there for you, with her family, she is a fine physician. You will be able to introduce your children to two others who are on the Earth who will be older, they are also named Michael and Rosie, also named for us too. Then you can remember that a Michael and Rosie will be with your friends, at your home on Cetacea. The Earth so badly needs these new tiny people more than it needs us, I think. I am so proud that my name will be carried by these innocent and beautiful ambassadors of survival, of trust, of belief in the future for both planets."

"If we can have another child, it will be Luna, boy or girl." I offered. Rosie looked shocked, but not upset. Last time we celebrated Rosie's birthday, she was forty-six. Probably it was too late. "It might be fun trying, anyway!" I said. Rosie gave jabbed me with a finger into the ribs, much to the delight of the children.

The time had come for us to leave, we fussed over one another until the last moment. Silky English announced "It is time to board the Cetacean ship, the de-orbit maneuver requires you to be in the ship within fifteen minutes."

Wendy herded us along towards the port, and handed me a small envelope. I wondered where she had found it, but had no time to acknowledge it, let alone open it. We passed quickly into the ship, out of Earth's reach, and looked back into Nantucket. Photographs were quickly taken from both sides, the hatch closed, and sealed. "Hard lock" said the new ship's computer. "Please relax, I will take care of everything from now on."

"Oh, if only that were true," said Rosie, looking with a critical eye at the less than spacious temporary accommodation.

"Mom, dad, I think you're going to love the colony, the people there are so nice. They have the best cocoa I ever had, and the most comfortable beds. Peter is right too, about the air, I mean. I could drink it all up!" said Andrea. She was trying hard to cheer us up, I looked at her and held her hand, trying not to shed a tear.

"Thank you darling," was all I could muster. Rosie did a little better.

"I think I'm going to need all of the good things the colony has, after all this," said Rosie, and then to me, "relax honey, we can't do anything for the next three hours anyway. Remember, one step at a time." She could tell I was nervous. Where did she get that sense of peace from, at such a time as this? "You should open your letter."

"What? How do you know...?"

"Just open it."

I opened a card with a holographic photo of eight of us just before the launch of the Nantucket. We all looked very fresh-faced, kids missing teeth, and the baby twins so tiny. Underneath was written in Wendy's handwriting, "*Credo, ergo sum*" with a series of symbols underneath, and signed with a W. "Show it to us then!" said Rosie.

"Dad, that writing underneath, that's Cetacean, it says... I, er, believe so I am? I don't know what language the first thing is, and I may have mis-translated."

"But you're right, darling," said Wendy, "I did not know you could read their language so well!" Just then the Nantucket emerged out of eclipse from the planet into sunlight, visible through a large porthole. The sun shed a fierce orange light. As the Nantucket slowly rotated, softer and more gentle beams seemed to warm her, and warm us. I could see a clear difference in Nantucket's appearance the last time I saw her, under the light of our own Sun. It was not the harsh brilliance of the Sun under which we were born. This cooler, weaker sun had safely nourished the Cetaceans and their flora and fauna. It was going to nourish us too, with luck.

Rosie said, "Oh, that light is so beautiful. Just look at how Nantucket gently glints. Our little piece of Earth now reflecting the light of a once-distant star. But the beauty is not just because of the light outside. It is because of the lights inside this ship, and inside Nantucket, the lights of life. *Credo ergo sum* is Latin, Andrea. '*Sic luceat lux vestra*' was my old school Latin motto, 'so let your light shine'.

"Yes," I said, recovering a little. "I for one especially need to remember to keep my light nice and bright for all of us, just like you all do for me. Thank you." I turned and grasped the kids' hands, and hugged Rosie. The ship slowly continued to maneuver far from Nantucket. As it slowly shrank, we could make out first Arcturus, and then our own Sun beside the glinting ship.

"Look dad, the Sun, I mean our Sun!" said Colin.

We looked in silent wonder. I had no idea of what the others were thinking then, but I wondered if the brightness of the lights inside the Nantucket would be enough to make a difference on Earth.

They needed to shine on the doubters, the skeptics, on the innocent, the guilty, everyone. They needed to illuminate Earth's future. They needed to offer hope. The populations of Earth would see our first transmissions including the Cetaceans only some years from now. I hoped that the planet was not even close to 34 Celcius when they arrived there, that Luna and her ambassadors would arrive in time to get the attention of 10 billion people, in time to make a difference. I hoped that they would not arrive, like we did, at the very brink of mammalian extinction. Then I remembered that this was not our problem, for now. Perhaps it would be in the future.

"Please prepare for de-orbital maneuvers including thruster activity" said the computer. I already missed Silky English.

"*Credo ergo sum*. That also means I trust, therefore I am" said Colin. I realized, with a start, just how much trust we had put into our hosts, as the craft's thrusters burst into action. De-orbit began with surprisingly large kick in the backside.

"Whoa!" said Colin, worriedly,"Is this right?"

"Whooppee!" said Andrea, "Here we go again!"

So, for Andrea, it was another ride in the adventure park, after all. Her enthusiasm reassured all of us. She deserved this happiness, I thought, just before the planet started to look much bigger and more dangerous out of the port hole.

Chapter 25

Nantucket's retreat

From the surface of the planet, we could see nothing but clouds. The light was slightly brighter in one direction, the only indication that there was a sun up. After looking around in the dull, muddy, misty immediate neighborhood, we walked into the underground bunker, on legs quite unfamiliar with renewed gravity. I suddenly longed to remove my helmet. The hermetically sealed oxygen mixture that I had become accustomed to suddenly seemed lifeless, sterile, artificial. I imagined the smells of weather, rain, mud, grass, life, fire. But we had strict instructions and we were not about to upset our hosts with utter stupidity, no "stopping to smell the roses".

We followed the tractor carrying all our Earthly goods, with a last look up, hoping that a break in cloud might reveal one of Andrea's mountain peaks, or, more fancifully, the sky, complete with the massive orbiting station above. It was but a mere fancy, the weather was indeed awful and it was daytime. We were either deep within cloud or ground fog. I was in a somber mood, a consequence of another life-changing decision, a done deal. I felt sure I would never see Earth again. I held Rosie's hand and squeezed through the gloves, without exchanging a glance. I could not look, not yet, I could not show I was frightened. She squeezed my hand in return, twice, until I looked towards her. She looked into my visor, and smiled. I smiled weakly in return.

As soon as we entered, the doors began to close behind us. We began to see a small crowd appearing in the dimmer internal light. Rosie and I were head and shoulders above most of the crowd. They were cheering musically, a sound unlike anything I had ever heard. It was muffled by our suits, it had an ethereal quality, quite enchanting. A couple rushed up to Andrea and hugged her, even though she was fully suited and isolated. They exchanged some musical language and Andrea beckoned to us to follow her to our temporary isolation quarters.

Within an hour of arriving, and having provided a little blood and other samples, I had cheered up greatly. "I don't know if it's the gravity, the solid earth beneath, the air, the new smells, the warmth, the new space we have, or just the fact that we are here and can settle. I just don't know... But I really feel as if my life has a new beginning, a new chance, new freedoms, new challenges."

"Me too, I am feeling really very relieved. I think it's all those things darling," said Rosie. We spoiled ourselves in the luxurious steam showers, warm soft towels, and ice cold fresh water. We changed into brand new soft towel robes. We were relaxing and inspecting our spacious and subtly different accommodations, remarking on the fact that this was merely an isolation room, when Andrea arrived with cups of steaming tea.

"Oh, my, this really is heavenly!" said Rosie, relaxing, spread out across a large and comfortable bed. We all just allowed the simple bodily comforts, the normality of existence on a planet, the hot tea, to relax us. "The best things in life are simple, and free. Well, almost free," said Rosie. "I would not change this moment for anything." We agreed, and eventually we all layed down and took a long nap.

An hour or so later, Colin woke us gently with a request, he wanted to try to see Nantucket in orbit, one last time. "I don't think we'll see that given that weather outside," I said. But obligingly, a female Cetacean's voice, or a translator program that sounded female, spoke from everywhere and nowhere inside our accommodation. It was a little worrisome to think we were being watched, but the voice explained that this was for our safety only during this decontamination phase. "She" then explained that a far infrared imaging camera was set up outside to get through the dense cloak of water and other molecules.

The Cetaceans seemed to anticipate all our needs. Was this due merely to evolutionary convergence, was it the result of an in-depth study of our needs based upon data in the cube, or some kind of telepathy related to Luna's skills? At this stage the question was of no consequence. I felt sure that we and Luna's people were in a fight for survival together. Circumstances on the moon had forged a tight bond of trust and understanding. If they had telepathic powers and we did not, so be it. There was little to be done, we would deal with any difficulties, if they arose, as they cropped up,

Colin was obsessed with his need to see our ship, and a feed from the camera was sent into our isolation room. During the first pass, a large centipede-like object passed across the camera's monitor.

"Hello again, my name is Eu-riel. This object you see in long-wavelength light is our space station", said a jovial female voice over some loudspeakers that seemed to be everywhere. "Please wait, I must calibrate the pointing mechanisms of the camera, now that we have an orbital fix, to find your Nantucket craft. I have received revised orbital data from Luna and the others. I will contact you again at the next pass." About an hour later, we heard her say, again from nowhere and everywhere, "This is Eu-riel. Please stand by for the next pass". Grouped around the monitor, the four of us saw again the station, followed by a tiny blip. "I have a fix on Nantucket, now I will process the images." After a second or so, a sharp image of Nantucket appeared. We watched it rotate, slowly, and gradually the images became more grainy, fuzzy, and noisy. We watched for some minutes. We could not take our eyes from the image of our entire world, a tiny microcosm of humanity, in the keen vacuum of space. The image dissolved into noise.

I felt uneasy at seeing Nantucket fade away into electronic snow, nothing-ness. My wandering mind produced some inchoate words, "so small, vulnerable, a microscopic thing, disappearing behind a few electrons... was our whole world... vulnerable... Galaxy so big... I'll miss her."

"Nantucket to Buxton, Nantucket to Buxton, please acknowledge." Ian's voice made us all jump, we had all been transfixed by the images. We had decided to call our small community "Buxton", the small town of 1500 people before rising tides reduced it to fifty or so, near Cape Hatteras lighthouse back in North Carolina. It would be some generations before the Cetaceans could boast 1500 souls, unless they were fantastically pro-creative and/or we were to discover pockets of other survivors. It might be even longer for Buxton, N.C., I thought, gloomily.

I blurted out to no-one in particular, "Where's the microphone, er, switch, computer, or whatever?" Andrea shook her head, smiling in disbelief at my ignorance, before she answered, smiling,

"Nantucket this is Buxton, we hear you loud and clear, we have been following you in your orbit. We are doing well, how are you all? Over." She had no microphone or any other device. I stood agape, but then felt rather stupid when we heard:

"Good to hear you Buxton, we are all well too. We have 48 hours before we de-orbit and head home. Over."

"We can see you from here, we have images of you passing overhead, you are really tiny compared to the station," said Colin, "we saw all the living and hydroponic pods and the motor, and the main cabin, so clearly!"

Andrea continued, "I find it a bit scary that much of the hope of two planets is contained in something we can see, something that we lived in, something so small. But Nantucket is a great ship. I think it's the ideas, the unborn babies and the messages they will carry that are the really big things." Rosie and I exchanged looks, I thought I could see both surprise and gratification in her expression. But she quickly turned away to hide a giggle. This usually happened when I wore one of my less attractive expressions. "It's the 'stunned mullet'" look again, isn't it?" I asked. She burst out laughing, nodding. The Australian expression left nothing to the imagination. I had to chortle a little. "Mom! Get a grip!" whispered Andrea with not a little stinging tone. "Take care of one other," finished Andrea.

"Roger that," said Ian, "you too, Andrea."

During our period of isolation, Rosie and I had some private discussions. After reassuring me that my mental clumsiness was definitely not early-onset dementia, Rosie felt that something was changing, had changed, in the "balance of power" between us and the children. Andrea had taken on a role of leadership quite naturally, Colin too in his own way. It was not just the decision concerning the return to Earth, but Andrea had also learned conversational Cetacean language. Several of her new friends came to the window of our quarters and exchanged smiles, waves and giggles upon her return to the planet.

I was surprised by how easily both Rosie and I had been happy to share responsibility. While young in years, neither Andrea nor Colin was a self-centered teen. Rosie expected significant rebellion any time, as a natural development phase. We would be wise to prepare for it, she said. Yet Andrea already commanded the respect of the Cetaceans naturally, somehow she and Peter had paved a path of trust. We thought that perhaps their straightforward honesty was a quality respected by the locals. The Cetaceans were happy that the first people from Earth that they would meet were children. The one thing their civilization needed more than anything was children, and lots of them. That must be it, I thought. Our kids gave them hope.

I wondered if children might be able to serve a similar purpose back on Earth. They might offer a young, unblemished, clear view of life, what might be needed to fix problems back home. After all, if Nicely could change so radically, surely so could others. I also thought of Nicely's response as being that of a child. Someone needed help, he had access to what they needed, he took it and delivered it. I decided I would have to meet the ex-Very Reverend, if ever our interstellar paths should cross.

I reflected on the wisdom shown by Luna and her friends. They had understood, much more than I ever could have, the importance of carrying their treasured offspring to Earth. This alone was going to be a message of intense and acute meaning, especially when the people of Earth heard of the state of the Cetacean race.

A day after our acclimatization, and still in isolation, we followed as Nantucket began de-orbital maneuvers. We also witnessed the Cetacean's next transmission to Cape Hatteras station, informing Earth of the return journey. Hatteras was targeted only at the Earth. The core message was simple, it was written with the help of Andrea and Peter. We were asked to comment on the message. "Just send it" was my reaction. It was encoded in our standard format, in English, Spanish, Chinese, in every documented living language on Earth. As the Nantucket prepared to leave, we heard the transmitted words in English, spoken by Luna.

"We offer hope, sent through our ambassadors traveling on the ship

Nantucket as she returns to Earth. We entrust to your care the children of our generation, precious new lives born after our own apocalypse. They are the seeds of a new hope for us, on Earth as well as on Cetacea. We are grateful, honored and privileged for the chance to share our lives with the people of Earth. Have faith, we are coming to you."

We all dwelt upon this statement. Belief, faith, trust, precious new life, I thought. How bright a picture of the future the words painted for a world condemned by skepticism and doubt, by short term gain, by consumerism, by mere convenience. "You know, *Credo* is such a beautiful word, compared to *Dubito*. Doubt is such an ugly word, with ugly connotations" I said to no-one, watching the Nantucket slowly but surely take her first steps home. "I cannot believe that generations on Earth, each in turn and with knowledge, put themselves ahead of their descendants. All in the name of 'doubt'." I realized I had unwittingly spoken into a silence left after Luna's harmoniously beautiful words.

"I'm sorry" I said quietly, to my family. I took a deep breath and said, more loudly, "Godspeed". It was aimed towards the Nantucket, my family, the Cetaceans, and the Earth, no matter the time or place.

"Godspeed", said Rosie, holding back tears. We embraced and turned to face the rest of our lives, together. "I could not do this without you" said Rosie.

"Nor me," I said clumsily. "I.."

"What about us?" interrupted Andrea, jovially.

"Yeah, what about us?" said Colin. "Come-on you guys, we have a whole new world to explore! Or at least, a whole new colony. The world will have to wait for a while, there's so much to learn right here, right now."

Chapter 26

BO'B's

I felt quite shell-shocked, we had progressed from orbit to permanent residence on an alien world within one week. It was fortunate that the Cetaceans had already connected the small computers we had brought from Nantucket to the feed coming directly from their lunar station, Hatteras Lighthouse. We received the first news from Earth within our first few hours in isolation. Rosie was very excited to hear from Earth. I confessed to Rosie that I was quite nervous about what Leon would have to share with us, things did not sound promising from his last communication.

"Good morning Nantucketeers! We hope all is well with everyone out there. Here is some more news for you all. First, we are doing splendidly well. Ria now has a degree in child psychology from Rice, she has been trying it out on me with great success, no less! I have gradually become a man of leisure, we live on proceeds from our books, and life is good. I am still meddling with motorbikes, my 250cc Yamaha now gets 120 miles to the gallon. OK. Now let's see... first some light entertainment." Leon winked. He looked very well, surprisingly so, I thought. There was a pause. We looked at one another, anticipating something, but we knew not what.

"The band, 'The Nicelies', now have a second hit. In fact, lead singer Brendan O'Brien experienced the meaning of the 'hit' first hand, as he passed out during the first London concert last week, in the middle of the new song. He got as far as the second verse of 'Take it Slow', maybe the slowest song I have ever heard, before taking a spectacularly slow nose-dive, mid-phrase, into a very excited and welcoming, predominantly female, crowd. It took the security people 25 minutes of wrestling to get him out! Afterwards, some of those security guys were not looking too good. Holy moly that made me laugh! It looked like a five hundred strong female rugby scrum versus the fifteen-strong New Zealand All-Blacks. Anyway, he was eventually recovered, rather roughed up and mostly conscious. Somewhat mysteriously, while he was fully clothed, his underwear turned out to be missing. This was discovered some time after as he asked his promoter 'Where's me f....g underpants?', in earshot of a live microphone. The band later swore that, while certainly drunk, he was not crazy and that he was indeed fully clothed before taking the stage. One of the band had a photo to prove it. This was not deemed suitable for public consumption, according to the band's manager. When later asked, O'Brien himself was wearing a smile on his face but claimed he was in need of some new clothes, and did the interviewer happen to know where the nearest Marks and Spencers might be. God, how we all laughed. I guess it takes all types..."

"Oh that is revolting," said Colin, "he must be at least fifty five! I could not think of anything worse than..."

"OK, OK!" said Rosie quickly, "We know, Colin, and I agree. No need to spell it out."

Leon continued. "But wait, the story thickens." Some uncontrolled laughter in the background. "Harry, stop, give me a chance, I'm trying to damned well read this for Mikey and Ian." Another pause. "So, reportedly, several tens of pairs of underpants appeared on gBay, offers over $1 million being accepted, each guaranteed as O'Brien's by DNA testing! Two of them were listed significantly higher in price owing to their 'pristine, uncleaned status', listed as being sold 'as-is'. At least one ad proclaimed that 10% of the profits would go to the Nicely numbered bank account,"

"I feel bad for the DNA labs that had to handle some of that," I said, "don't they have anything better.."

"...and as for those two, the Nicely monks have gone to ground now somewhere in Afghanistan. Apparently there are some very palatial caves there. Centuries and centuries of conflicts led to a rather profitable line in 'cave improvement' for creative entrepreneurs. Some have secured remunerative contracts with satellite TV networks over the years, with shows such as "This olde cavern " or, for the really high profile terrorists, "Location, location, location" continued Leon. He was indeed looking well, I thought, much better than last time. We all needed a good laugh from time to time. "Some of the caves are reportedly modeled after wonders of the world, one has a 'Victoria Falls' toilet, another a 'Marie Antoinette' bedstead.

"Anyway, enough of that for now. The deliveries that Nicely has been sending just keep coming through. There is nothing the 'authorities' can do about it short of invading the Swiss Banking system! Various western groups have demanded access to these accounts, but no group that actually is in power will have anything to do with it. Just imagine what else they would find, opening up that little den of iniquity. So that will not happen. Anyway, estimates report that Nicely's work has saved something like 140,000 children already. Now that is what big money *should* do! Along with many others, I am really beginning to like the guy.

"Oh, and there is yet another amazing (or I should say 'amusing') thing, the stories here just seem to go on and on. This past Sunday was Fathers' Day. Amazing sights were to be seen outside the Houses of Parliament, the White-House, and other major seats of government worldwide. Thousands of fathers and sons (and perhaps more daughters!) showed up with shaved heads and monks' habits in peaceful protests. There was a shortage of tonsured wigs in the UK. The be-habited monks asked that the Big Banks and Financial Institutions follow the Nicely Father and Son, by actually helping somebody, somewhere, at some time, just for once. Now in London itself, O'Brien had sobered up for a short while and was the well-received mascot of one large 'band o' merry men' marching along the Mall, towards Parliament. That was until he dipped out for a 'quick one along the way' at a pub he was familiar with. A reporter for the perennially dull and unimaginative Daily Telegraph wrote that, when downing his alleged 'first glass of the morning', O'Brien was wearing nothing at all under his habit. When asked of his sources, he only said they were 'close to O'Brien'."

We laughed with tears, as we then watched a bizarre short video clip of a few dozen monks wrestling with English bobbies. Apparently they were only 'trying to get a close up view' of the inside of the pub, wanting to buy O'Brien a drink. The headline read 'Turning wine into water?' Leon began his old peculiarly infections laughter, and I could not help but join in after all these years. When he had recovered, he began again. "Even better, there is now a new chain of high street underwear, called 'BO'B's Vanishers, for that special occasion'. Seriously. Can you believe this stuff?" He wiped his eyes and tried to pull himself together. He finished this episode with

"My oh my! I'm sorry. The English have a saying that 'Bob's your uncle and Fanny's your aunt'. I don't think I would want that BO'B in my family!"

Chapter 27

Not even 'yesterday's news'

Leon took a large drink of water, a few deep breaths, and succeeded in pulling himself together. He really enjoyed sharing these trivia, but obviously the next installment was not going to be quite as amusing. "Well, anyway, I am also supposed to give you of some 'real' news, unfortunately, so, here goes." Clearing his throat, Leon started reading loosely from a monitor in front of him. Images appeared in a sub-frame of the news items. "Martial law has been declared in Las Vegas County by the Feds. Neither water nor power have been cut off as yet, the population of several hundred thousand contains hard-nosed libertarians for sure, but many more innocents who are just trying to live and let live. The Nevada National Guard however has split into two factions, and you can imagine what that might mean. The Feds hold the north end of Las Vegas, then there is a no-man's-land north of the strip. In the south, the hard-core group of self-appointed outlaws, police chiefs, National Guard sympathizers, hotel owners, are now heavily armed. Their weapons include several fighting vehicles and even surface-to-air missiles."

"Jesus," said Rosie.

"Several illegal flights arrive daily at McCarron airport carrying people from all over the world. Some just want to gamble. Others want to exercise their freedom to do 'whatever they want', it being their 'right' under this country's constitution or that. Yet more simply wanted to witness this historic standoff for themselves. The US Air Force and Nevada National Air Guard has so far not intercepted such flights, but things are going to get ugly soon. The governers of Nevada and Arizona have refused to parlay with the US President or the UN. It looks like a farcical version of a classic State or City vs. Federal stand-off, if only it were not actually real and so serious. It's a hell of a mess. I fear for the children."

Leon's words left us feeling hopeless. The nature of time and space, "space-time", made any attempt to do anything on such a short time as months, weeks, years, decades futile. If ever there was a time I felt we needed a "sci-fi time-warp", it was now. I wished we could send instantly our remarkable story. How could the wealthiest and most powerful strains of humanity remain so unaware of the deadly cost of short-term self interest? How could they not see the cost of hanging so desperately on such a thing as a "constitutional right", something meant to protect people, at the expense of future human life? Then I remembered again, this news arrived twelve years after Leon had recorded it.

Here and now, at tau Ceti, things were desperate, with a species on the edge of extinction. Here and now, the destructive societal myopia was no longer relevant, it had died out with the lethally changed weather. Instead, the remnant society had no choice but to re-build, patiently and with mutual nurturing. The Cetacean's natural world had been decimated. It seemed to me that the biggest challenge was patience, patience spanning generations. This was clearly in very short supply in Las Vegas. I realized, wryly, that this was nothing new in that particular city. Perhaps that city was lost, already.

"Rosie, God help me, but I am so frustrated, angry, I feel totally powerless. I feel cheated that there is nothing I can do, nothing I can say, that will have an effect on those back home for more than a decade. We've come all this way, we have new and unique knowledge, experience. We can perhaps even provide some wisdom. We have a revelation to share with our world. The revelation will surely persuade world powers to change direction, give back some of the future to the next generations. But I am frightened that by the time any signal is received, things may be too late. I wonder what Ian, Wendy, Luna and friends will find, back home."

"Michael, I know what you mean, it is difficult to give up the feeling that we have some control over what we care about. Remember though that generations of people who cared about the future Earth had to be denied it by those in power, those skeptics, deniers, bent on consuming through business-as-usual. We were two of those people before this all started, before you found the Cetacean signals. What's really different for us here is that Earth is no longer in our sphere of influence. We just can't help in the way we'd like to, in the way we were used to. But this is not new either, remember how big the Earth used to be in days before technology. It took weeks for warships in the Americas to receive news of the defeat of Napoleon, they were still fighting a war that was over.

"But what I really want to say is this. In psychology one of the most difficult things to treat is a deeply ingrained belief that people can control things. This is a fallacy and a delusion. Out here, we have simply the 'here and now'. Our now is here. Not there." Of course, when looked at like this, psychologists had been dealing with the delusion of control for a century or more. I realized that my struggle was no different from people under the delusion that they had control of things around them, their very lives.

"Honey, I think I get what you are saying. In fact, I feel free-er knowing that I do not, absolutely cannot, have control. You have reminded me of my own limited and distorted view of things. The slowness of the speed of light, the large distances, showed me explicitly the meaning of the delusion of control. I suddenly feel compassion for people suffering from this delusion, but entirely unaware of it, back home. After all we've been through, I should have known better. Much better. How are you able to see things in this way, I mean, it cannot be 'just' textbook psychology?"

"Well, I think I have learned a lot from life, from our experiences, but my background does help me see things for what they are, and I do not mean physically. I think of it as just *awareness*. Awareness is not something a physicist would grapple with, but it helps me to see a different side of problems, the side that makes us aware of our own limited understanding and capabilities. This does not mean we are to let this awareness cripple or disable us from making progress. No, instead I think it helps us to make better choices in the quest to make better progress,"

"I am pleased about two things." I replied. "First, I am happy to leave the really difficult subjects that you have to study to you. Second, I am really glad you are my wife, helping me blunder my way through this life. We have a crazy language. I do the "easy" "hard" science, you do the difficult "soft" science.

We laughed. "You know, our language is so plastic... how many languages are there where 'hard' means 'soft', and 'soft' means 'hard', you know? I just love it!"

"Except maybe when it comes to poached eggs?" joked Rosie with a bright smile.

I chuckled along. "But I wonder if all languages are as weird as English seems to be?" We held one another, and started exploring more contradictions in English. We thought that maybe the mixed Roman and German origins of words often led to these kind of strange English contradictions. But then I realized I knew nothing of the 'soft', or was it 'hard' subject of etymology? Or should that be semiotics? I quickly realized I did not care. But after a while I decided I might study this stuff, in the long-term, including the new Cetacean tongue. I would, after all, have a lot of time, and I could not do any astronomy from beneath these clouds.

I got up, felt the solid ground under my feet. This was something I could grasp a firm hold of. I celebrated by walking around for a few minutes. After a drink of water, a visit to the toilet, I returned to bed. All I knew right here and now was that I loved Rosie very much. I kissed her hair. But she was already asleep, making her soft purring noises. I thought maybe I had bored her to sleep. She was able to sleep upon hearing the latest news from Earth. If she could do it, I should be able to as well. Instead I simply let the purring comfort me again.

Chapter 28

Afternoon tea

We both awoke to a large afternoon tea made again by Colin. Our sleep cycles were slightly "off". The Colony had developed a night/day lighting cycle to match the outside conditions, using artificial light. "My, this looks lovely!" said Rosie. "Where did you find all this stuff, it smells amazing, these are all Earth things, surely it is not Cetacean food? Can I try it?"

"Of course mom. What I did was to look into our archives for the recipe and examine the makeup of all the ingredients. The Cetaceans have a kind of '3D food printer'. Once I had figured out the computer interface, all that was needed was some protein, carbohydrate, fat, fiber, minerals, and Bob's your uncle!"

"Just what does that mean then?" I asked.

"It means something like, 'hey presto', or 'behold', I looked it up. It came from some English politician's favor for his nephew, or something like that."

"I see. Very interesting. Well, let's sample the goods then." I said. The melted butter on the scone was perhaps the most delicious thing I could ever remember tasting. Rosie and I looked at one another in astonishment. "Wow, this is incredible! The tea too. Let me see, it's Earl Grey with some black tea too, right?" I said.

"Almost, I put in 'Lady Grey' and black tea. Is it OK?"

"Darling, it's wonderful," said Rosie, "you are so clever. Thank you."

"You'll need some strength for what I have planned over the next week!" said Colin. "Wait and see what my hamburger and fries will taste like tonight." Our eyes widened. This was perhaps the kind of shot in the arm I really needed to begin to face the future here. I remembered something about secrets, hearts, and a man's stomach. My stomach rumbled loudly. Rosie and Colin laughed loudly, I blushed, and laughed. To recover, I asked

"Colin, this is wonderful, how did you make the interface work? That sounds very challenging."

"Well, the Cetaceans helped me of course. I started thinking about it soon after our arrival on the moon, before we knew what we would deal with. I did manage to find a way to port our software to theirs with a very fast universal subroutine that simply handles all operations, and is transparently clear to both systems. It worked first time."

"Colin, I don't remember anything like that back on Earth." I said, surprised.

"No dad, there isn't anything like it. That's why I just sent it to the Nantucket so they can start using it. They took one of their 3D printers too, and so they can try Italian, Greek, Indian, American, any kind of food they want."

"You are a force of nature... there isn't anyone quite like you, darling," said Rosie, "come here and let me and your dad give you a big hug."

"Am I not getting a bit old for those hugs?"

"You're never too old for that," said Rosie, "come here!" She ruffled his hair, I poked his stomach, and he giggled like he was a three-year-old again. It had been a while since our rather serious little boy had done that.

Chapter 29

Terra, Firma

Our time in isolation over, the introduction to the whole colony was very informal. We were greeted by a friendly mature couple, arm-in-arm, outside of the isolation room. With the help of Andrea we were able to express our deepest gratitude to them. They did the same to us, they were so genuinely thankful for what we had done that we were humbled by their graciousness. How I had longed to have such grace in the midst of my own life's challenges, over my many years battling away for tenure, for success, for personal rewards. Rosie and I would later speak of our recognition of some of the finest qualities we strove for as humans, in the Cetaceans.

We were led slowly through the underground complex to our new home, we were to live in Luna's old quarters, and the children would be adjacent. I felt a little short of breath, but the period of slow decompression in isolation had helped, I was not about to keel over, not in this 0.8g gravity. The "houses" reminded me of middle-eastern buildings, perhaps Mediterranean, a mix of sloped, domed and flat-topped roofs, in a small 'town'. The feeling of being outside was enhanced by some clever lighting, spreading diffuse light from a blue, partly cloudy sky. We heard the ringing of a bell, we smelled trees and their blossoms, there was a light occasional breeze. Yet echos told us that we were inside a large structure. The contradictions were a little disconcerting, at first, as if two of my senses were telling me slightly different things.

"Oh, this is a lovely place," said Rosie, "it reminds me of, oh, I know, the Mosque of Cordoba, but with a higher ceiling, and many more little buildings inside of it."

"Yes, you have it!" I said, remembering the expansive interior of the famous Moorish building and its remarkable niches, arches, columns, nooks, churches inside. We looked at the vaulted ceiling some tens of meters above, wondering what light sources there were that gave one the feeling of being outside. "Maybe with some of the pretty buildings of Santorini?"

"Well, I think you might be pushing it a bit there, but I know what you mean." replied Rosie.

"Excuse me please, this is to be your new home, if you approve" said our male friend.

"Mom, dad, this was Luna's house! I have been here a lot! It's lovely inside, come and see!" said Andrea.

"Andrea and Colin can live just here," said the female, "it belonged to my dear friend now with Luna, on your Nantucket."

"Oh, mom and dad, you should taste the 'oranges' and other fruit that grow on the roof of this house!" Andrea spontaneously embraced the couple and skipped over to her new dwelling. "A house just for me and Colin! Come ON Colin, let me show you!" she said.

The home for Rosie and I was a small white dome-covered building, it looked so natural in its environment that you might even miss it upon a first glance. The children were to occupy a smaller dwelling with a flat roof and a garden on the top. It was, like many of the buildings, set upon the sloping floor of the cavern, houses were set at various heights throughout the colony, as dictated by the rock. We entered our new home, and were greeted by a truly tiny person, who bowed, and asked us all to sit and enjoy "breakfast". The ceilings were low for us, I did not quite need to stoop, but needed to be careful. Colin's wizardry had allowed the Cetaceans to cook up a New Orleans-style brunch, beignets, chicory coffee, and all. Our welcoming committee wanted to retreat, but we insisted they join us. With trepidation they tried the coffee, but not the blackened red-fish.

They left us soon, wanting to let us simply "ground" ourselves, a curious phrase, but a welcome one for space travelers. Colin remarked, "Ah, that reminds me. You know, we need to decide on names, English names, for our new friends."

"Oh no, we have to use their own, proper names," said Rosie, surprised.

"But mom, they have asked us to name them, just like we did Luna, that's why they did not give their real names," replied Andrea.

"Yeah," said Colin, "I think we should. Andrea and I scanned a few files on our cube and looked for something a bit like Luna. We came up with *Terra* for the female, and *Firma* for the male. What do you think?"

"Oh, now that *is* clever!" said Rosie. "They are also very nice names too. Terra, Mother Earth, and Firma, solid, strong. How appropriate."

"Good," said Andrea, "because they already have adopted those names, they know what the names mean to us."

We laughed and settled into a couch by an open arch. We heard giggling outside. The tiny person came in to sit with us. "Hello, my name, my new name is Go-li-ath. Goliath" he said proudly. "I am named, named after a giant famous in Earth's culture. Andrea tells me I am a giant among the Cetaceans, a giant in character, in my life energy, and I am pleased to meet you." I could not help but see Andrea's point, both Rosie and I smiled at this. "I hope you like the brunch?"

The kids laughed, we said yes, but confusingly then shook our heads at the nerve of our children. The giggling outside restarted, even louder. A small crowd of youngsters had gathered outside. This was an unexpected start to our new lives. Faith, hope, humor. What next? I had a feeling that the children would have more to say about that. "So much for a short 'grounding', how about we 'ground' ourselves outside with these kids?" said Rosie. With Goliath, we wandered outside for some new introductions.

Chapter 30

Unspoken Words

We shared daily reports with Nantucket as she accelerated towards Earth, out of the tau Ceti system. The weather pattern outside had settled into hurricane-like conditions soon after the Nantucket's departure. This was, according to the locals, now the post-global-warming "normal" weather. Previously the weather had been temperate, much like northern Scotland had been back on Earth. We reported how we had ventured outside, after all, it could not be that bad, could it? We badly wanted some "fresh air". We went against the strong recommendation of Goliath. He looked on us very disapprovingly, as we donned our outside weather gear. We became soaked throughout within thirty seconds. So, instead of soaking up wind-driven water, we spent much time inside the Colony, soaking up knowledge and enjoying mutual question-and-answer 'outdoors' meetings with the locals. In this place it was easy to imagine Aristotle with his peripatetics wandering among the relaxed atmosphere of the village, a place thirsty for the exchange of knowledge. We compared our respective palettes and menus, and even shared the recipe for the synthetic Shiraz wine that Colin had produced, at half its usual strength. As it turned out, the Cetaceans uniformly preferred the golden Tokaj, Colin's latest efforts.

The news from the Nantucket was good, we were delighted to hear that the flight so far was deathly dull, exactly what was needed. We continued to feel relieved to be on firm ground, able to live as "normal" a life as possible, here on Cetacea. Life continued in this fashion for many weeks, the weather monitors showing 150 kph winds on average, visibility of mere meters, on average. Neither I nor Rosie were progressing much with the language, we did not need to. After all, "necessity is the mother of invention".

After four months had passed we received our daily report, this time from Wendy. "We are well within the interstellar medium, outside of the heliopause – the direct sphere of influence of tau Ceti. The Nantucket is behaving nominally, we have gained a speed of 15% of the speed of light, right on the money. Our daily routine involves mutual education and learning. Gaia, Tara, Phanes and Luna just gulp in our culture and history, the names they have adopted are from their research on fertility. I like Tara's adopted Druidic name. It seems Cetaceans have a soft spot for the romantic. All three women are beginning to show, I don't think I have seen anyone treasure their unborn in the way these women do, and Phanes cannot do enough to help them. He assists with their daily exercise and stretching routines and monitors all their nutrition. He instructs me on the delivery of Cetacean babies, we learn the women's anatomy and physiology together. Ultrasounds reveal four healthy babies, we have some months before delivery. We are all doing well,

"Barrie and Peter are also devouring knowledge of the Cetacean culture. Ian and I have difficulty making them stick to their ordinary learning. Luna has become a kind of unofficial teacher, as she uses her phenomenal learning ability to teach the children about their own culture and history. Barrie and Peter speak to each other in the Cetacean language, we wonder if they might be hiding things from us, the little monkeys!" said Wendy.

Aside from the last phrase, Wendy's report was delivered in an unusually matter-of-fact fashion. Her usual passion seemed missing. We wondered if something were wrong. "Why is Wendy so, errm, unanimated, do you think?" said Rosie with just a little concern, "She really does not seem herself to me. Is she hiding something perhaps? I cannot believe that, we have always been so open. Maybe she is just, well, tired. I don't know."

"I don't think we should worry just yet, but there is something a little odd in her behavior, I agree. Remember that the time lag has been well over the tens of seconds for "conversations", and so we all end up delivering news, or non-news, with no more conversing. Also, no news is good news, as they say."

"But they *would* tell us if something were wrong, right?" asked Rosie. "I mean, would you?"

"I would." I said with unconvincing confidence. We had a little time to think about these communications. Of the reports, Wendy's did seem to stand out. Ian made us laugh with his take on The Nicelies news, Peter impressed us by reciting the opening scene of Macbeth in the Cetacean tongue, to much applause, and Barrie showed us how to play Gaia's flute-like instrument which allowed her to sing at the same time. The instrument seemed to be designed to resonate naturally with the Cetacean's voice. It could not work like an Earthly flute, it required so little breath. It produced harmonies naturally, Barrie demonstrated by singing some fifteenth century plainsong which induced a special "drone voice" from the instrument, not a drone or a voice, something in between.

We sent a reply with much applause for the children's performances, with cheerfulness as well as an optimistic report of our own period of learning.

We were approached the next day by Goliath. "I have for you a message from Luna. It was 'inside' the last transmissions, it was lost, no, hiding, inside the message, within the transmission. There are several of us who can use our minds to share feelings, information, experiences. I am one such person. I felt Luna active when you heard the messages. I did not first comprehend the message, but I have reviewed it and I do now understand.

"Luna says that she notice a change in Nantucket, no, she means the people Ian and Wendy. Cetaceans and children are the same. She asks for help from Rosie as sy-kol-o-jyst. She will try sharing mind experience during the next messages. Rosie is to undergo training."

"But, what does she say, is Luna very worried?" asked Rosie.

"A little, not much. Please she asks for not to worry. But she does need Rosie help."

"Of course", said Rosie, "I'll be happy to start any time."

We looked at one another, and held one another, in silence. "One day at a time," Rosie reminded me.

Chapter 31

The news of the world

The Cetaceans called a 'town meeting' in the village square, to be led by Terra and Firma. The first order of business was to share news about the re-population program. First, Terra asked that all pregnant women step up and join her. Of the thirty five females, fifteen collected around her, showing various stages of gestation. After a brief period of applause, something of a ruckus then occurred in the crowd, as an upset male was pushing people aside and looking intently into the eyes of others. Firma stepped over and began some undecipherable discussions with the individual. The male was stopped on his way to the pregnant women.

"What's going on, Andrea?" Rosie asked. Neither Rosie nor I had made much progress with the language.

"I think that the man who is upset wants to know something about being a father. How to be a father." Rosie raised her eyebrows. "No, sorry, about *who* is a father. Surely that does not matter, all that matters is that there are fathers and mothers. Mom?" Rosie and I exchanged glances, and I began to giggle. Phrases such as "it's the same the world over", and "people never change" came to mind and gained a more universal meaning. After it was clear that the situation was going to be resolved peacefully, we laughed together, and explained to Andrea what the story was. Later we had to explain our reaction to Terra, who did not understand our amusement. She remained puzzled. Apparently this was either a very unusual event in Cetacean relationships, or Terra's intervention was unusually successful.

"She is pregnant, she will have offspring. We will determine genetic makeup of all offspring later. That is all." It seemed the latter was indeed the case.

Second in the order of business, Firma reported on some new planetary scans obtained from a recently rescued and recommissioned artificial satellite. One engineer was charged with recovery of whatever satellites she could, this was the first. All that was needed was to transmit several recovery codes, eventually the satellite would be at the right attitude to receive them and react. The data hinted, very slightly, at a possible area of activity on the surface. He reported that the orbital spacecraft encountered breaks in clouds, but these were rare, and only occasionally had the spacecraft scanned the same region twice. So the evidence for changes was necessarily rare. So this finding was significant. Images conjured up on a wall-screen showed changes in the configuration of old dwellings, from satellite scans weeks ago to more recent scans. However, the extreme cloud cover allowed data from only two very recent passes. More convincing were data from a thermal imager, showing accompanying ground heat. The area was known for its planeto-thermal activity though, so again this was inconclusive. The Cetaceans seemed wholly unconvinced. But then Colin exchanged a few words that seemed to garner interest and a little enthusiasm.

I looked toward Colin with a questioning expression. "Dad, I just asked if a thermally active area might be a natural choice for refugees, even in a warmed climate? The emerging water would be boiling underneath and would contain minerals, it could be used for boiling food, killing germs. Also natural shelters with warmth would protect from the rains. The Cetaceans seemed to like my argument, so they are going to direct more satellites to scan the region, but the weather is atrocious so they are not hopeful of results. It seems an expedition might be tried. They believed that we might be well equipped to aid in such an effort." This was very welcome news to "However it is about 1000 km away and a sea crossing would be necessary."

I was impressed again with Colin's insight. "Colin, you amaze me with your breadth and depth of knowledge, as well as your language skills." I also liked the idea of an expedition. It was comfortable in the colony, but I still felt like I wanted to do something useful, in our own sphere of influence. "A reconnaissance/rescue mission might be something I could really contribute to. After all, it was hard to be an astronomer given the climate conditions outside," I said to Rosie. She reluctantly agreed that for my sanity, it might be a tonic. She too would like to go. I decided I had better start exercising, to convince everyone of my fitness for a trip. I needed to get out on the surface.

Rosie and I chatted at length about this. She reminded me of something obvious. "Oh, but remember honey, you have terrible sea sickness. You'd never get across the water crossing. I'm sorry." My enthusiasm had gotten the better of me. We discussed what I might contribute, even if I could not get to the region of interest.

Over dinner, our family talked about the possibility of venturing out again onto the surface. We would be ideal candidates, or so we thought, being bigger and presumably stronger, and none of us was needed to nurture precious new life. So far as we knew, the human race was not facing extinction, not yet.

Andrea then reminded us of something equally important. "Mom, dad, it's interesting. I just realized that we have become settled and accustomed to our new home, and this news seemed like 'local' of 'family' news. But in fact, we were just presented with the news of the world, the whole world! There *is* no more news, here and now, at least. That's it. I mean, because of their global apocalypse, this is both a very big and a very small world at the same time. It shows how very important every single person here is, doesn't it?"

"You could not be more right, dear," said Rosie, "both of you always amaze your dad and me with your different insights. I don't know what we would do without you."

"Luckily, you don't have that option, mom!" Said Colin with a broad grin.

Chapter 32

BO'B's your uncle?

"Hi guys, this is Ria Adamson, M. Psy., bringing you the news of the day from Earth. Leon sends his best but he is away at some world event in Berlin. It's a bit of a long story, but then you have lots of time sitting around, enjoying the high life, so here goes.

"First, we are all well, I am seven months into the pregnancy and lil' Rosie seems to be doing well. I had some blood pressure and diabetic issues, but these are being taken care of. My feet are up and I now eat meat, cheese and lettuce. Well, mostly, anyway. I miss the bread most. But so far so good, a little goes a long way, and the local Jewish rye bread is excellent and low-carb. Michael is performing tricks at the mall, he often grosses three figures an hour. I never expected him to be "normal" and "boring" given his parents. But he is impressive, and his schooling is going very well. So Leon and I remain happy with him. He fusses over me like you would not believe, will not let me do anything. That's why I am recording this transmission while he is outside!

"As to Leon, well, he has gotten quite intrigued in the new youth movement, "BO'B's your Uncle". I don't mean he wants to join as a youth, no, he's following it. He believes it to be something really new and perhaps important.

"The father's day event this year seems to have a lasting effect on kids, sons and daughters, everywhere. It turns out Nicely Jnr. was a rebel and a total pain to his dad all his life. According to files leaked by Nicely Jnr.'s uncle, Nicolas Nicely III, the Reverend sent the spoiled and highly petulant child to a military prep school at age eleven, sure that his son would "come around" and see the light of his father's message. Quite the reverse came about. Some years ago, having drugged the school security guards, guard dogs, and at the precious age of fifteen, he led a vigilante expedition to Wall Street and managed not only to get in, but to halt the proceedings there for two days! He dumped some kind of instant nausea gas into the totally sealed building's AC system, for sudden remote release into the building. It took the police two days to track down the cartridge embedded in a nook so cleverly placed that it must have required significant insider knowledge. The Wall Street Journal reported the incident as biological warfare and the United States went to a higher DEF-CON level, treating it as a serious terrorist threat. Security tapes identified nothing unusual, it had to have been an inside job. A really excellent inside job.

"Well, two weeks later, after several groups had claimed responsibility but had been shown to be unconnected, the same thing happened at the London Stock exchange. The authorities remained totally baffled, and would still be today if not for the frustrated Uncle Nick III.

Meanwhile, over at Junior's school, The Principal had noted that, oddly, their security officers had been "assaulted" on exactly those weekends of the stock market attacks, by unknown groups, using horse tranquilizers. Nothing seemed to come of it. He dared not inform the Board of Governers for obvious reasons, there could surely be no possible connection, could there, with the bio-attacks? Even if there were, his fitness as Principal would be in serious question. But relentless Uncle Nick III then leaked a local police report in which, having graduated with honors from the prep school, Jimmy Jnr. walked into the local station and claimed he was behind the whole thing. Of course he was not taken seriously, and was told to go away, and "stop wasting police time". Being just fifteen, the police could not do much anyway, his father would be responsible in the state of New York anyway. The real kicker was Jimmy Jnr.'s claim that the deathly "biological agent" was nothing less that the highly concentrated essence of the toilets from two of Wall Street's favorite and most frequented high-end restaurants. The FBI concluded that this the child was obviously looking for attention from his father. However, they were "very keen" to speak to the boy,

"Well he got his father's attention alright. The unofficial story is that the Reverend was called into the White House to "explain yourself and your wretched offspring." Nicely was handling himself with the usual panache of self-assuredness of a Man in His Position, when the Chief of Staff blurted out. "Oh for God's sake man, save your bullshit for the outside, here we need truth, save your lies for the pulpit." When the President Herself walked in, Nicely had to confess that indeed difficulties had arisen between himself and junior.

"No fucking kidding," said the President, "have you any idea where this demon seed of yours has put us? We cannot prosecute since the story he has is just too embarrassing, incredible, stupid. We cannot prosecute because you will be the one responsible, and you are one of the main reasons I got here in the first place! Jesus Christ, I cannot believe this shit. You either have one of the smartest or dumbest goddamn kids on the whole planet. And right under the eyes of one of the best military schools in the Country. Christ Almighty... What I am to do with you now? I would not ask you to conduct a bus anymore, let alone a presidential campaign. Get out of my office!

Ria continued: "The bottom line is that something about this kids' rebellious years has fired the imagination of his generation. There is a rally of the BO'B's your Uncle movement in Berlin this week, hundreds of thousands are expected. Leon could not resist and so I gave him leave to attend. I will bust his ass if little Rosie decides to pop out tomorrow! Well, he is hoping to meet The Nicelies as well as the Nicelys – if you get my meaning. Father and son are rumored to have migrated to Switzerland where they are still on-the-run.

"OK, that's it for now. God bless everyone."

Chapter 33

Action at a distance

"I can't do this psychic connection thing at all, I simply cannot find any kind of connection other than physical. I have had zero success, nothing. I wonder if humans have anything like this capability at all." Rosie was despondent, feeling like she had failed. I held her close and reassured her:

"This was always a shot in the dark honey, remember? You have not failed. Not at all. To have tried without success is definitely not failure." She smiled, unconvinced, but was grateful for my attempt. "You know I am right about this?" She nodded.

"But Luna asked me to help, I have to help, I want to help, but I just can't do it."

"Mom, you ask if humans can do this at all. How about we try again, but with me, dad or Colin?" asked Andrea. "After all, how much of our medical knowledge would have been gained if we gave up at the first experiment? You also know very well mom, we are none of us the same! I think we should all try."

Rosie looked up, exhausted from her days of frustration and smiled. "You're absolutely right honey, let's talk to señor Goliath again. I think it is time for another try, another subject." That night, Rosie fell asleep during the very first paragraph of 2001: A Space Odyssey. She usually waited until paragraph five, at least. One of my favorite books and movies of all time, she would read it when she suffered from insomnia. It simply was not her thing.

Colin's experiment produced instant results, following a total failure by myself and some partial encouragement in Andrea's case. Rosie was absolutely fascinated. Colin explained that it was no effort at all, and that he had inklings of this as Rosie was undergoing her frustrated trials. Images flooded across from Goliath to Colin on the first try. The blind tests were absolutely conclusive. Until we could understand and further exploit this new sense, Colin was our "high bandwidth" receiver of information from the Cetaceans. He sat down and watched Luna's previous transmission with Goliath and Terra. He immediately understood Luna's concern. We wondered why we had not thought of this before.

"Mom, dad. Luna has witnessed a sudden change in the way in which Ian and Wendy interact with the rest of the crew. Ian pretends rather poorly that all is well, and Wendy does not even bother. She is down on herself, worried, she keeps to herself. She is sleeping fourteen hours at a stretch, she is uninterested in the kids. I could almost see this happen like it was in front of me. Incredible."

"Oh my," said Rosie amazed, "poor Wendy, these are classic depression symptoms. It is not change-of-life, the change is just too fast. This is related to a different change in brain chemistry, some trauma perhaps, or just biochemistry. We will have to probe further, carefully. This is going to be hard with such a time- and distance- gap. We owe it to them to find out what is going on and solve it. I will talk to Wendy myself, as best I can. They are receding fast, I will have to act fast to be effective. They are as yet a few percent through their journey, during which they will need Wendy. So much time left..." The sparkle in Rosie's eyes had returned.

Rosie spent several hours studying the cube's clinical psychology library, preparing for the next scheduled transmission. "You know Michael, trauma is the mostly likely match to Wendy's recent psychological history, so far as I can glean. I suspected this from the beginning, but I wanted to eliminate many more possibilities. Turning to the transmit/record mode, she began.

"Hi everyone, this time it's me, Rosie. You know I am still the Nantucket's psychologist, even though we are separated by time, distance, speed, red-shift. In our latest communications, we noted that both of you show that something has changed, emotionally, psychologically, maybe even more. I am here to help, just as I expect you to help with our medical issues. I am pleased to say, that as of now, we have had not even a cough. But remember, we are the best we have for one another. I have to talk to you openly, but I cannot. So the best I can do is share my concern and ask you to explain to me what is going on to cause this change. You must understand and remember that the number one risk of this mission is, and always has been, associated with psychopathy. So I'll remind you of something that has and does inspire us every day, something that makes a big difference. They are your own words- '*Credo ergo sum*'. These words took us down to the planet's. It was a rough ride, made easier knowing that you were there for us."

Late the next day Rosie received a reply that shocked us. "Hi Rosie, we really appreciate your words, and your offer, things have gotten a little tricky in the last few days, and indeed I am struggling. Two things, first, Nantucket's motor showed an anomaly, we had a small burst of high energy particles in the cabin that looks non-lethal, but we don't know the resilience of the Cetacean physiology or their ability to protect their unborn children. I am observing them very closely for signs of radiation poisoning. The anomaly is of the form that Mike and Ian discussed at length, it was extremely short in time which seems to have helped to save us. We had a warning, but no engine shutdown. We continue to accelerate."

"Oh God," said Rosie, "that is really horrible. I guess that she and Ian have taken it upon themselves to talk, but that they don't know how to deal with the kids or the Cetaceans. They need to do that."

"So," said Wendy, "we have not yet spoken to everyone about this event. Perhaps you can give us a little advice on how to do this."

"Of course," said Rosie under her breath.

"Secondly, I myself have developed symptoms of an auto-immune disease, which is fast acting, and really wearing me out. I have made a temporary diagnosis of Lupus. Ian and I have looked over the Nantucket's cubes for treatments but it remains to be seen if we can manufacture the needed medications. I arrived at the diagnosis about a week before the motor anomaly, but symptoms were obvious now I look back, for a month or so."

"OK, a serious breach in radiation shielding, and a chronic and very painful disease. That's too much, and I am not sure Ian is the best at handling such things. I guess we will find out." Said Rosie. "I will recommend immediately telling her kids, Luna and friends about the anomaly. Problem sharing is good. I will also recommend that Wendy ask Luna and colleagues to look over what is known about Lupus. I will instruct Terra to ask the local geniuses here on Cetacea to investigate Lupus in our cube database. You never know, there may be the possibility of a cure or at least something palliative that will really help. They are going to need our help, and it will not be long before we are so far away in time that I may end up treating a psychological problem many months out of step with the condition. I don't have a good feeling about that, I don't even know quite where to begin."

"Just one thing at a time, darling."

"Yes, yes. So, first I think I will recommend a higher dose of antidepressants, but I have to be careful. Wendy must be able to think clearly, it will not be long before she is called upon as a doctor, nurse, midwife, pediatrician. To deliver those kids safely, she is going to need her wits. Maybe the best anti-depressant will be her own kids, she needs to re-engage with them, and to engage completely with the mission goals. I wish I were there."

"But then you would not be here, for us," I said. "you can't be a mother to the Universe. Just treat one world at a time."

"Damn Einstein and all those speed-of-light nay-sayers," said Rosie.

"You can't argue with the laws of the Universe, even though I admire you for trying," I said, "it shows how much you care, I'm proud of you."

"Well, having failed at the psycho-communication thing, I do know that, in this situation, I can do some real good. I must help Wendy soon, I do not want her to suffer more than she has to."

"You're a real fighter, aren't you?" I said with admiration. "I honestly think the laws of nature might break one day, faced with the force of will of people like you."

"Hmph."

Rosie's plan of action was initiated with gusto. We soon had the resources of two worlds looking over one of the most resilient and nasty auto-immune problems plaguing humanity. I wondered if the disease stood a chance against such odds, or if such things were simply beyond all our abilities. For the time being, my money was on the Cetaceans, their experience and skills. No matter the outcome, I felt sure something good would come out of this. Then I remembered that this was precisely why we had been sent into space in the first place, in hope of finding new solutions to old problems. Unfortunately for Wendy though, she had become our first challenge, and it was going to be personal.

Chapter 34

A break in the weather

The pilot stepped out of his machine and into bright sunshine. His face broke into a big smile. His flight of over five hours had been extremely dangerous, the heli-jet was well over design limit in the atmospheric turbulence, and the relief on his face was obvious. He was happy, but obviously drained by his battle to keep the aircraft aloft against the horrific weather.

Ten minutes later, the same young man stood before another meeting in the town square, washed and brushed, finishing up a quick meal and a drink, but otherwise in flight garb. This was too important a report to allow any unnecessary delays. We listened intently on the auto-translate system, we had used this too much because we wanted to learn the language. But this was a serious meeting, and so we wanted to understand and follow the Cetacean reaction with no ambiguity.

"The flying was extremely difficult, physically and mentally. There was no particular 'turbulence' because it was all turbulence," the crowd looked very serious. "But I was able to find a layer where it was reduced. I had to rely on inertial navigation, our nav-satellites have been ignored for so long that drifts in attitude and orbit rendered them too inaccurate." Murmurings grumbled within the crowd. "I arrived at the target area under terrible weather conditions. A landing was out of the question. But I surveyed the area as best I could until I realized I was getting very tired. None of us has yet had a chance to study the data even though I was transmitting all the time. Our radio communication satellites are operational but very spotty. So we will take our first look now, at the heli-jet's own computer records, which have just finished downloading."

Against the wall of the largest building we saw some footage from within the cockpit of the aircraft. "This is my helmet camera, as you can see, it was rough going." The crowd took a collective deep breath. I was astonished at his ability to fly the thing at all, the images were all over the place, I could make out almost nothing. There were loud bangs as the helmet struck the cockpit frame, again and again. I had never seen an aircraft subject to such forces. "Next I'll show you the stabilized reconnaissance images we have all been waiting for, I have not seen these myself." The space went deadly silent, I could hear only the sound of the stream.

We watched as a scene emerged intermittently between clouds, a murky, steamy, watery-looking region with areas of uprooted and downed trees, mixed with a few resilient or collapsed buildings. It looked like a disaster area. The crowd did not react, they had lived through this, it was all too familiar. The aircraft then descended slowly, and the images, though containing gaps, remained rock steady. The thermal source seen from space was obvious, a blurred infrared image was overlaid transparently on the visible images every few seconds. The aircraft made two complete circular arcs around the region of interest, and then ascended into the clouds.

"I saw nothing obvious in those images," said the pilot, "did anyone else?" No response. "Very well. The next thing of course is to build the three dimensional images from this sequence, so here we go..." A three dimensional rendition of the same scene appeared in the space between us and the pilot. The crowd closed in around the image, looking intently for something, or someone. "No, step back a few paces, the images will then be easier for us to see," said the pilot. We all moved backwards. Neither Rosie nor I could see anything but desolation. After some time, on the third rendition of the sequence, some excited discussions arose, the auto-translate could handle one voice at a time, so we could not pick up anything sensible. The image was rotated, it was focused in, and out again. Still nothing. Some excitement broke out as Firma tried to point out a feature that seemed interesting. I looked to Andrea for a possible hint of the conversation, but then the other voices dropped, and we could again follow the argument.

"No, my friends, we should not expect to see one of our kind in these images clearly. Just because we do not see someone does not mean they are not there. You see, the rendition we have made assumes that the scene does not change during the time it takes to make the 3D image. The camera on the aircraft has to move about one tenth of a circle to build up the 3D rendition. But here, in this area, we see a blurred volume." He stopped, paused, and declared, "This is precisely what we would expect to see if things were moving. It is like trying to scan a patient who cannot stay still. Can we see one or two images please, perhaps those taken closest to this area of most interest?"

"Yes of course" replied the pilot. We waited as more commands were sent, and looked again at the wall. We could see three things that might, just might be humanoids. The crowd gasped, they so wanted them to be just that. But the images were too amorphous, too vague.

"And the second pass, please?" In another moment, another rendition appeared. There was no blurriness in the same region. "OK, so this is somewhat encouraging, if there were people there, we might expect them to move around to attract attention." The small crowd took a moment to digest what they were seeing, and the rationale they had been given. Suddenly, they burst into applause, which was followed by a hum of conversations. God, I hoped they were right. These people needed some really good news.

Skepticism was obviously a human condition. Even given my newly-found "*Credo*", I could not help but recall the faces of women, even of Elvis Presley and the Virgin Mary clearly "identified" on images from Mars during the period of the Rovers. One simply had to be careful when faced with too much hope, and not enough data. People too often saw what they wanted to see. Were Cetaceans any different?

Chapter 35

Berlin

"Hi everyone, this is your friendly neighbor Leon reporting direct from the city of Berlin." He was having to shout very loudly among a boiling sea, full of young people. "As you can see behind me I am part of a huge crowd gathered here at the first international meeting of ByU – BO'B's your Uncle! I have been promised a meeting with BO'B himself later. Also, those not-so-nice-Nicelys are rumored to be in the area. A huge police presence silently looms over and around us, small regiments of Polizei cavalry and troops are all around. ByU is devoted to the mission of the Nicelys. ByU's sole aim is to kick those propagators of consumption and profiteers of conflict where it hurts them most. By sapping money from them, and using it to save those in need. This mandate is labeled "terrorism" by The Authorities. Hence the Polizei, horses, tear gas canisters. I prefer "altruism" myself.

"The Reverend himself has made a significant move from the Old to New Testament in posting one simple message. The words

Blessed are the meek, for they shall inherit the Earth

appeared overnight in enormous letters. They were written in English and Hebrew, on Mount Eremos. The message was so huge it was only possible to read it from high flying aircraft, or from space. The intended receivers of the message are only too clear. How many spacecraft do the poorest nations on Earth have in orbit? How many nations have enough wealth to worry enough to spy on each other from space? The message was read almost immediately by the CIA, MI-6, KGB and Israeli

Secret Service. All these agencies suffered leaks to the press, within an hour. The words were written using bills, in many different currencies soaked in honey. They were entirely unusable and effectively stuck where they lay, baked by the Sun. It took some weeks to get the trees out of the mess.

"Nicely and JJ remain silent, they naturally have taken no credit. No-one knows where they really are, it is all just rumors. But no-one believes anyone but those two could could be responsible. The amazing thing is that all the bills were never released for circulation, the two of them seem to have supporters stretching into Treasury Departments worldwide... Some in the media are assessing what the sum of all the leaks and the cooperation that the Nicelys seem to enjoy, really means. Prominent commentators say it is a warning that they have resources to de-stabilize the world's economies. They ask themselves and us to imagine what a flood of free money would do to the world.

"Well, anyway, aside from dislocated refugees of global warming such as the Pacific Island Nations, the only nation that has formally signed on to the ByU manifesto is Cuba." He waited significantly, as if allowing for us to recognize what this might mean, historically.

"OK, so right now we are waiting for a speech from the Mayor of Berlin. He was the biggest of fish we could get from the traditional powers-that-be, 100% of big business leaders refused to attend in spite of all-expenses paid invitations." He paused while the crowd around him reacted with their traditional gestures with fingers and other things, pushing, shoving and jeering. We were impressed with the sheer variety of lewd gestures at hand.

"See that guy there, in the red had- British!" said Colin. "It's in the finger action." How he recognized this I will never know. Colin's cultural studies were certainly diverse, deep, perverse or all of the above. We could identify the cultural origins of at least two other individuals from their characteristic finger gestures. This was clearly an international event.

After this group of international sign-language cognoscenti had calmed down a little, he continued: "After this, we will hear about the origins of another 'major terrorist group', Greenpeace, and similar environmental organizations. I'd better sign off now, it looks like things are starting up." He was jostled violently and carried bodily by the pressure of the rambunctious crowd. For his own safety, he climbed up and the video clip ended with Leon "surfing" on his small cauldron of supporters.

"I'd love to be there, dad!" said Andrea, "I think it would be absolutely brilliant, with Uncle Leon, BoB's your Uncle and the Nicelies, and all those young people! I'd shave my head like a monk, and..."

"You would do no such thing!" I said rather more aggressively than I intended. "A daughter of mine? I should think not..., shaved head indeed."

Rosie put her hand to her mouth to suppress a laugh, in vain. "I'm sorry," she said, "it's just so nice to see a 'normal' interaction between father and teenage daughter,"

"Oh mom, dad! Come on. I am almost fifteen, pretty grown up already, and.."

"Let's just listen, shall we?" said Colin, obviously annoyed. Rosie was laughing still in the background, and shaking her head.

We watched as the broadcast changed from the crowd scene to a pub, dark, dingy, drab, smokey. Then, in a very poor imitation of Richard Attenborough, Leon was seen cautiously moving as if through undergrowth. "Well, here we are, we are not sure, but we have been informed that this is a lair frequented by the rare bird Brendan O'Brien. It is purported to be one of his more famous "watering holes". In fact, rumors have it that many of this particular species visit this particular oasis, providing them with life-giving sustenance. The black liquid can keep a Brendan going for a full 24 hours..."

"Oh my aunt Fanny, what an old hack! Honestly, does he think he's being funny or something?" Rosie said. "He even makes you look funny, sometimes," she said, turning to me. I offered my insincere thanks.

"Shh!" said Colin, taking it all in, "It's really interesting." Leon continued,

"I can't say where we are since we are sworn to secrecy, for the protection and good of the local wildlife." The camera followed Leon into still darker cubby with a couple of shabby unshaven men sitting and drinking what looked like pints of Guinness, surrounded by at least six empty glasses.

"Good evening! You must be Leon" said the first man in a strong Etonian or Charterhouse accent. I am pleased to introduce a chap I have known since prep school, this is my friend Freddie, Frederic Ogilvy. My name is Bob, Bob Bryans. Also known as Brendan O'Brien, don't you know?"

"Delighted to meet you old boy" said Freddie. The camera turned to Leon,

"You, er, you... "

"Indeed," said Bob, or Brendan, "I know, it's a little white lie that we would not like to become known, it would disappoint a whole generation of youngsters, of my, er, nieces and nephews, if you like. Ha ha ha."

"You mean, errm, you mean this whole thing, it is a complete act?" said Leon, blundering his way through to his own very good "stunned mullet" expression. "You're not actually Irish, or a, a drunk, or any of .."

"I say Barry, bring the chap a drink, he has won first place in the 'plain and bloody obvious' contest!" shouted Bob to the barman.

"Nah, he can come over an pay hisself like everyone else. After all the prizes that fella's won over the bloody years! Interstellar signals. Huh, no bloody use to anyone."

"Oh don't mind him," said Bob to Leon, "he's just part of the local fauna, old chap. He doesn't bite, not hard anyway."

"Well, I'm sorry to disappoint you on your first question old chap, guilty as charged, it is an act. A good one though, I think," replied Bob, "As to the second question, the jury is still out on the drunk. But at least I come by the acting honestly. I am still paying off loans for my education at RADA you know, the Royal Academy of Dramatic Arts."

It was like watching some absurd British Farce, the next thing I expected was the vicar to come out of a cupboard holding an actress' bra, and an retired, gouty British Army Officer to club him with a piece of lead piping. Like Leon, we were initially a bit too shocked to laugh. I for one thought the whole thing could have been staged by Leon himself. But Leon could not be that good an actor. No, this was real, it had to be! Bob continued

"The 'underpants incident' however, was entirely genuine and unanticipated. A feisty lot, those British Gals, you know! But please forgive me, and sit down and do have an actual drink. Herr Ober." Bob winked at the camera, or maybe the camera-woman, seeing the twinkle in his eye. He was good, 'dangerously charming' as Rosie said afterwards. She did not intend it as a compliment. The bar-man grudgingly came over with three more pints, poured lovingly over the last twenty minutes. "There y'are y'English bastard."

"It's a term of endearment between Barry and I". Returning to the camera-woman and then Leon, he continued "So, you have both signed the binding contract over those video rights, correct?" A yes answer emerged out-of-sight of the camera.

A few seconds passed. Leon looked even more astonished, he began to smile, and he said "you were in on this?". The camera turned to reveal Ria, taking off sunglasses and scarf, smiling and waving. We could hear Leon in the background. "Oh my God, you're 7 months pregnant, you can't fly. What the hell are you doing? This is nuts!" Leon had to make sure that Ria was well, and that the baby was doing fine, that she had not over-stressed herself. She simply smiled and placed his hand on her tummy. Leon's face was alight with pleasure.

"Oh doesn't Ria look well mommy!" said Andrea, "I suppose pregnant women, the healthy ones anyway, always look so well." Rosie nodded, and the clip continued.

Ria set the camera to record the three men. Leon sat down to try to conduct an interview. At first he could not stop smiling, chuckling, but he pulled himself together. Ria explained to Leon in front of the camera that this was expressly only for transmission out of the solar system. He was clearly a little surprised and frustrated by this, he was perhaps hoping for a "scoop". But both Bob and Freddie admitted they were greatly honored to be selected for transmission into space. They also were delighted to meet one of the discoverers of extraterrestrial life.

From behind the bar came "Extraterrestrial bloody life, I'll believe it when I see bloody it, that I will!"

Freddie shook his head, and then explained that, as Bob's manager, he would do most of the talking. It turned out that they both worked commercially as the Nicelies, he was financially independent, but they were under the umbrella of a much bigger 'underground organization', "...If you get my drift?" said Freddie. The organization had been in place for a century, with its origins in post WWII Britain. It operated under extreme secrecy. No one was ever permitted to meet anyone other than their first contact, and no real names were ever shared. Much of the activity used principles adopted in top secret activities of various Secret Service agencies, from the period known as the Cold War. Yes, there had been defections during the Cold War, but most of these were strictly planned and staged beforehand. In Britain, for instance, damage to National interests was never significant, and the Russians always paid for the defections in the end. How did Leon think that the Soviets were finally beaten? He did not believe all that Reagan and Gorbachev historical bluster, did he? The Berlin Wall that marked the historic events was merely a few hundred meters from this bar. They were sitting on top of one of the best kept secrets of all history. Bob and Freddie raised their glasses, winked and said "sláinte".

Freddie continued, "But, of course, today our covert operations are best done using social media, but in a very sneaky fashion. Our organization is very *re*-actice. Pro-active work tends to be too easy to infiltrate. We take advantage of situations, like the Nicelys, and try to capitalize on it. Hence, BO'B's your Uncle!" (A clink of glasses). "This is just the most obvious of many ways in which we undermined, worldwide, the 'evil empire' of rampant consumption, denial, skepticism.

"But enough of us, more than enough, actually. Let's make sure we get today's job done, before someone breaks up our little party, or before our party really gets going, shall we?" said Bob. Freddie took on a more serious air. He could not give away strategic or even tactical goals. But, looking into the camera, he said, straightforwardly.

"This is a message to for the Kerr and Cowling families. We are greatly honored to be a part of this new effort to re-align humanity with the natural needs of the planet. We wish you good fortune in finding help at tau Ceti. We hope we will not need your help, but many of us feel that we will. Godspeed to you all, and your mission. You must know that while our work involves an almost impossible fight for long-term survival at the expense of short term profit, we are making progress. You are not alone. BO'B's your Uncle is a most unexpected and welcome turn of events, we are attracting youth across the planet, by the millions. We have infiltrated deep into all areas of established government and commerce worldwide. But it is the youth that will win out ultimately, because this world is for them and their children. Things are changing for the better. We hope to be among the first to welcome you all, upon your return."

Return. To Earth. This was the first time in months that I had even thought along those lines. I was still not sure that I should actually believe this peculiar story, it could be just a huge joke. But I did not think Leon cruel enough to talk about return, without meaning it, so it could not be a set-up, could it?

"Oh, before I forget. My name is not Freddie, I am not his manager, he is not Bob, he is no-one's uncle, not even a monkey's, and I have no aunt Fanny." Bob, Brendan, or whoever this was, smiled broadly, winked, raised his glass and said

"Well, very good, but I now have a concert to do. Sláinte!"

"Oh no, BO'B is a fake then?" asked Andrea sadly.

"Oh no, indeed," said Rosie, then with a smile, "I really think he's the real thing, the real deal, darling."

"Wow."

Chapter 36

Hope and strength

The colony was buzzing with activity and excitement, many had volunteered to take on the expedition to attempt to find survivors in the geothermal area of interest. Firma called those interested to the meeting place. Under the translator, we witnessed an amazingly short meeting in which the teams, modes of transport, route planning, contingencies and communication modes were discussed briefly and then set. It was cut and dried within ten minutes. Six were to leave. Both I and Colin were needed for our size, strength, and something about us offering hope. Colin explained that Terra and Firma, Goliath and one other who's name I did not catch would also come along. A pilot would take the team to an area containing an engineering research depot, last noted to contain valuable all-terrain vehicles and equipment.

"Darling, this is going to be very dangerous, are you sure you need to go? You cannot be considering taking Colin?" Rosie was concerned, if not downright upset.

"You know the answer Rosie, to both of those questions. Our friends have need of us, we are about twice as strong as any other here, and sheer strength can make all the difference in a situation such as this. The fact that they have asked tells me that we are truly needed. Peter and Andrea led us to the planet because of their particular physical attributes, and that turned out well. Four of the Cetaceans with four unborns are on their way to Earth to help us. This is the least we can do. Also, do you fancy telling Colin that he cannot go?"

"I understand of course. But you should understand too, that I simply had to ask. I love you and Colin so much, I don't know what I would do if..."

"But mom," said Colin, overhearing, "I understood Firma's words, language, what he was really saying. The translator missed some important things. What Firma actually said was, "We believe in our new friends, they are our hope, our strength."

Rosie put her hand to her mouth. "I suppose we all need something to believe in. But this will have to change."

Chapter 37

Beatitude

The news from the home world was, as Leon said on the next transmission, "Getting a bit complicated". Leon explained that he was delving personally into the Bob and Freddie story, and was coming up with absolutely nothing. Leon was always a supreme hacker of the internet. So this was very significant. Rosie and I agreed that either the thing was a complete pantomime, or it was absolutely true.

I was just hoping that Rosie's assessment was right, their story offered hope, to think that there was an old underground agency at work trying to restore the Earth to its naturally balanced state. The agency's activities would be carefully disguised, subtle, hidden. But to be able undermine the entire Soviet Empire? This did not seem credible. Surely Brendan, Bob was joking about that, his smile and wink, but I could not tell... It was all so strange.

I relaxed in our dwelling with a small glass of the very good Shiraz. Leon's words interrupted my peace. I tried to distill his message's essence from the lengthy, entangled reports. I wanted to be able to summarize the communications for Colin, Andrea and Rosie, who had volunteered outside the colony, taking advantage of a drop in wind speed to work with high tensile windmills. They also tended to the few crops that could withstand the gale, strategically protected by dense hedgerows of the toughest low-lying trees I had ever seen. The roots must have burrowed meters deep, down under the top-soil.

Later, we gathered for an update on Earth's news. Terra and Firma would in turn give us the most recent report from Luna. Rosie and the kids had been outside for a total of two hours, venturing outside, roped together, in fifteen minute periods. After some cleaning up and refreshment, we sat down in our house with Terra and had afternoon tea, with English muffins, butter and jam.

"OK lazy-bones, why not fill us in on the latest from Earth?" asked Rosie.

"As far as I can tell, things are pretty much the same, with one or two notable changes." I began. "First, the BO'B's your Uncle and other organizations, while getting much more support, have not pressed home any advantages gained by their earlier actions. There have been neither arrests nor further 'in-your-face' antagonism. Leon thinks this is compatible with ByU's overall strategy, they are in it for the long term, there is no rush. The youngsters do get edgy, wanting to see quicker action, but the organization seems to keep things peaceful by assigning carefully planned tasks to them. Some are sent to work in rebuilding housing, some to work in their form of "finance", others are trained in machinery, nursing, engineering, all using available educational channels except where the work is deemed highly illegal. The biggest threat to ByU is infiltration by thugs, giving the authorities excuses to portray them into a violent organization, and infiltration by "double agents". Both of these worry Leon, but so far, so good, he says. He does not know why the organization seems so stable, but maybe the Nicelys and ByU have really buried themselves so deeply in all areas of society that the sheer weight of numbers, combined with the pure humanitarian mission, simply avoids such problems. Any violent or obviously subversive agent would not be tolerated. There are definite movements in support of ByU everywhere that it is known, across all demographics.

"Leon believes that the re-distribution of wealth to the top 0.1% of those in the western world, rationalized and enabled by right-wingers in the early 21st century, is finally going to really bite them, and hard. There simply are not enough of these people, even with their outrageous monetary power and absurd and immoral rationalizations, to overcome the obvious need to defend the future. Your typical French Canadian, Taiwanese, South African or whoever, has realized that big corporations have stolen the future from everyone in the name of "business". Yes, many people supported these businesses, but most now feel that they were deceptively hoodwinked. Fairly or not, many now see the ultra rich, trying to keep their riches, as the main proponents of the Skepticism movement. Most of the billions of people worldwide know only too well, although too late for many, that short term tactics "do not a strategy make". They are systematically withdrawing money from traditional businesses to those that fight them, as well as those that promise longer-term sustainability. Leon had signed off with the beatitude, "Blessed are the meek."

"It is about time," I thought.

Chapter 38

Las Vegas

"Leon also reports that stakes had been raised by groups of libertarians and others, who are epitomized by the hold-outs in Las Vegas. These pockets of die-hards, pretty much found worldwide, are determined to 'live free or die', freedom having a meaning that seems even to include their right to destroy the future for everyone else. They deny flatly that, against all rational thought, their "harmless agenda of convenient consumption" has had any effect on the trajectory of Earth's biosphere. They therefore have a right, no a duty, to protect the rights of those like themselves who grew up consuming, and they were damned well going to die consuming. After all, they had done 'nothing wrong' in their own eyes. Indeed, they had been materially damaged by these meddling enviro-creeps.

"I will not inflict on you again my views on why these people are ethically bankrupt. Instead I will let Leon explain." Leon's voice started.

"I have to report that their world, as well as that of the super-rich, is changing. Two weeks ago the water supply to Las Vegas was cut. The power was cut three days later. Roughly half of the population of downtown Las Vegas has emerged over the last ten days, delivered mostly on ancient Courtesy Shuttles from the major hotels, to no-mans-land. The rest have dug in to defend their rights.

The State Department of the USA was clear about its approach to the "LV problem". Leon played a recording of a spokeswoman, who stated that "Federal authorities know that there are weak, helpless people in Las Vegas, as well as the power mongers. We have had to make some heartbreaking calculations. We chose the lesser of the two evils by adopting siege tactics, knowing only too well that those in power in LV will take care of themselves there first, sacrificing the poor. Our siege will break the back of these rebel leaders. They cannot survive without water, power, food. Half of the population of Las Vegas has realized this and capitulated. We are hopeful that the rest will soon surrender to common sense, and help to save as many of the lives of the weak and defenseless as possible."

She continued, "Yesterday, however,it seems that the people in power in Las Vegas let their supporters down. They took captive an emissary of peace, someone sent in simply to educate the Las Vegans about the rest of the world. They kidnapped the nephew of the President of the United States. They demanded water and power. They got both, but not quite in the form that they had requested. Water cannons, tanks, were brought to the very edge of The Strip bordering no-man's-land. Water and food was made available on the federally controlled side. A few thousand more people surrendered shortly after, leaving a hard core of tens of thousands in the city. The refugees reported that there was no way in hell that the hardcore "authorities" there were going to give in. They believed the death toll in Las Vegas had climbed to over 1,000 as the heat and lack of potable water and sanitation were taking the biggest tolls. Piles of bodies were believed seen in cemeteries around town. The death count is climbing still. Unfortunately those power mongers have made their decision. The siege continues in spite of provocation by occasional snipers at the border."

The faces in the room looked grim, the atmosphere felt heavy. Then Terra spoke.

"This might be a low-tide mark of your planet's crisis," said Terra, with grave concern. "Yes, you have lost tens, even hundreds of millions of people. Yes, the planet's path is fixed as it must be, following the dictates of universal physical law. The laws of thermodynamics are not subject to the opinions of senators, parliamentarians. I am sorry we could not have made contact many many orbits ago, when we might have helped you avoid the warming crisis on Earth. But if I am right, things will improve. I recognize parallels in our own societal evolution. I remain hopeful. For us. For you. I feel Luna and all our friends will make a big difference on your Earth.

"Perhaps now I can report from Luna? There is some news from the Nantucket."

"Please do", said Rosie, "but please oh please, we need some news that is good."

Chapter 39

Lupus

Terra began. "Luna, Gaia, Tara and Phanes have worked without break, to combine our joint knowledge of auto-immune problems in the two species. Immune systems are perhaps the ultimate expression in nature of mathematical 'complexity'. They are so complex that, even with our computational powers, there is very little we can do from pure analytic theory. Instead Luna and the others searched our database of immune system computations, which revealed emergence of Lupus-like pathological behavior in our own immune system under several circumstances. They did the same with data for the human immune system. A careful computational search of our two histories revealed a correlation of occurrence of the disease Lupus with a particular combination of provocative agents. Given this commonality, knowledge of the agents involved, Gaia has now identified a molecular pathway for progression of the disease, suggesting a possible treatment."

"Oh that is such good news!" said Rosie, obviously very relieved.

Terra continued, "Wendy is studying the action of Gaia's new agent in vitro. We will try the in vivo treatment only with extreme care, only after Wendy has assessed possible toxicity."

"That sounds worrisome," said Rosie, "I suppose there is nothing to do but try it, and see what happens?"

"Not in the patient, straightaway, at least. We can do some computations and try to see how any agent might interact with the human biochemistry, but our knowledge of that is woefully incomplete, even now."

"So, I guess that is still good news?" asked Rosie.

"Oh come on mom, I think it is," replied Andrea, "Wendy has good reason to hope now."

"Of course darling, you are absolutely right. The word is *'credo'*, after all!"

Chapter 40

Wendy

Three weeks of testing different synthetic agents had passed. Wendy was working in tandem with Gaia to run many combinations of molecules in vitro to try to identify possible clinical candidates. It was painstaking work requiring enormous patience. Wendy was on some pretty heavy-duty pain killers, devised by herself and Luna after some further joint research. During this period, Ian was getting more and more worried about Wendy. She had become pale, large, dark circles under her eyes, and her temper was becoming short. He would try to comfort her in bed at night, gently holding himself against her, the warmth often such a comfort. But there were times when she could not abide being touched, she was obviously still in chronic pain, with periods of acute myalgia. He also felt that her work load was antagonizing the disease, and vice versa. Her situation was not sustainable, something had to be done. He was trying to decide how best he might intervene. He exchanged some written communications with Rosie as to how he might delicately express his concerns. She advised him to do just that- express his concerns, his feelings, not to judge her but simply let her know what he seemed to be seeing.

Ian stepped into the "lab" area, and said "Wendy, here's some fresh tea. Might I suggest you take a break, we could sit and have a quiet cup together, you are looking rather.."

"Damn, damn and damn!" said Wendy. "The T-cells are still way too active for this particular agent, they are reduced only by 10%. We need to reduce them by a factor of two, at least. I don't know if we're ever going to find this. Every time we get a good response, there is some kind of predicted organ toxicity. At this rate I'll have to give up on my kidneys, my lungs, or something. This is incredibly frustrating!"

"Wendy, sweetie, I see that you have been working very hard and I so want you to find your treatment, you deserve it so much. We never thought this would be easy. I wonder if you should take a break from..."

"It's OK for you, Ian. In the meantime I am in so much pain! I'm sorry, I didn't mean... Oh God.." she burst into tears. Ian took her gently to his shoulder and delicately massaged her head, he could feel the wetness of her tears on his neck.

"Oh no, how I wish I could do something to help. I feel so bad. I wish I could take your pain on myself, I really do, if I could do it. I feel pretty useless."

"It's OK, Ian, I know how much you care. Let me tell you something I learned from a patient many years ago. He was really suffering, and he said to me, 'you know Wendy, this disease sucks. But I would never want it to develop in a loved one, a friend or one of my own family. Rather it be me. It's easy being the patient. It's much harder being close family- they don't know what it's like, so they guess the worst.' I agree with him. But, I just don't know if ever we will find something that can help. Maybe I'll just have to wait until we get back home. But my symptoms are getting worse quite quickly. I just don't know what to do."

Peter stepped in, bringing some sugar for the tea. "Mom, dad, listen. This is important. Barrie and I have been looking into the Lupus files in the cubes." said Peter. "We also looked at our medical profiles from our lab work on Earth. There might be another option."

"Oh my dear kids, you are so kind, but..."

"Mom, listen. I really think we can do a mini-stem-cell transplant, from one of us" said Barrie.

Wendy looked utterly shocked. "Oh baby, that is a very dangerous procedure, we would be taking enormous risks, also we must look to antigen matches and all manner of things."

"No mom, remember we are completely isolated out here, we are almost living in a clean room. Yes, the bacteria in our hydroponic areas are healthy and there is some risk from them, but this is not a germ factory, like the hospitals on Earth. We have looked at our antigen patterns. Peter and I are almost perfect antigen matches with you, we are both 23/25."

Wendy looked at them both, crying, shaking her head. "Come here, both of you." She hugged them tightly, and kissed their heads, one-by-one. "Oh my sweet children, you are so thoughtful and kind, but you don't know what you are getting into. I'm sorry, I can't ask you to do this." I could immediately tell that she knew that the kids carried a potential cure, that they carried the building blocks of her own immune system. But she also knew that their healthy systems might just restart her own system and could really cure the increasingly debilitating condition.

"We have been talking to Peter and Barrie, as well. We all believe this is the right thing to do, your condition is worsening" said Gaia. "We think you should do it. I am happy to be trained to be your primary carer, I think we will be able to succeed. The children are extremely fit, they will not experience any risk themselves, none at all. "

"But I am the one who is supposed to be taking care of you, all of you!"

"How are you to take care of others if you do not take care of yourself first? I have read of this problem with your doctors and nurses on Earth, it is a very common thing. It is an honorable problem to have, but it is a problem!" said Gaia. "We will all be just fine, you have trained us all well. If we cannot adapt and help each other, our futures are doomed anyway."

"We want to do it mom", said Barrie.

Wendy and Ian converged on the children, and embraced. Gaia joined them. Wendy would not let go of that huge weight pulling her down, not yet. But there was a feeling that someone had lightened it a little, a very little. She so wanted to believe that this damned disease would be cured. She began sobbing and smiling and holding her children very tightly, even through the myalgia. She began to realize that she had been carrying far too much of the emotional load for her crew, and she noticed that her pain had momentarily receded, just a little. "I think I'd like to sleep now, I would like a story, I think."

"How about Peter Pan?" asked Peter.

"That would be lovely."

Chapter 41

A very good day indeed

We had arrived by aircraft at a base on the "other" side of the intervening body of water, some 150 kilometers from the thermal site of interest. The scout pilot had dipped below the very low cloud deck there to avoid the worst of the turbulence, at considerable personal risk. She was firmly reprimanded for this, warned never to do it again, her life was far too valuable. By chance, when her new images were inspected, they had revealed that a civil engineering depot appeared fully intact. The logs showed a large repository of equipment and supplies had been placed there years before. There was no sign of any activity, and it appeared to be fully intact. We had been flown to this depot in the best weather we had seen to date. It was indeed the worst flight of my life, so I was very shaky when we stepped into the depot, greeted by the sight of a full inventory of hardware.

The land-cats were dead, we had to install new batteries and clean out the engines with steam. In anticipation of such problems, we had brought power packs, wind generators, lights and a variety of other hardware in pods under the aircraft wings. The cats were driven by gas turbines, part of the old order. But they were what we needed. Any chance we had to find survivors for the Cetaceans had to be taken. Solar power was obviously inaccessible to us, so we installed the ingenious expanding wind turbines, which began generating some 100 kilowatts of power in no time. Hurricanes are useful, sometimes. We had a long journey ahead, over territory that was previously known only to be dry. But goodness knows what was there after the shifts in climate. We tried not to anticipate trouble, but some caution was in order, and we would have to prepare carefully, before continuing our expedition. So we settled in to cook a large meal and sleep overnight in the warmth of the newly reheated hangar. We left in good spirits, after a filling breakfast of porridge, at first light.

The cat had been grinding away for hours in dim light, which was the best light we could expect under the dense cloud decks. Eventually it became dark, and the headlamps penetrated the continuing deluge out to about ten meters. Our speed was limited to a mere ten kilometers per hour. The cats traveled in a group of three. When one became stuck, as was inevitable, the other two pulled it free. Each had a pilot and co-pilot. Goliath and I shared number three. Eventually it was our turn to lead. My knees were almost around my ears, I was glad that the controls were entirely manual, no feet involved. Colin and a new friend, Juno, were in number one, and Firma and Terra the other. We had all volunteered for the mission, and had argued vociferously to keep our group tightly-knit. The Cetaceans wanted all six places, as a matter of honor. But Terra had reminded them that no genetically viable person involved in re-population could take the risk. Goliath was deemed too old, Terra and Firma were put into a small group of people who had tried and failed. They were also more mature than the median Cetacean survivor, and were therefore in a lower priority group. Juno was a master of many trades, negotiation, medicine, psychology among others. Her collective skills were deemed critical to this particular mission, even though she could readily become child-bearing.

I had been exposed to the grinding of the tracks of the cat over the rollers, the whining of the turbines, the noise of the wind and the rain on the cabin, for upwards of a day. Goliath and I had just changed roles, I now drove, he was observer, lookout. In spite of this exchange, the familiar, almost deafening repetition of the noises had dulled my senses towards drowsiness. I was brought quickly to my senses. "Danger!" said Goliath. I stopped. "This is a temple, it would not be good to crunch into it, very bad, er, bad luck, I think," said Goliath.

"Thanks, thanks Goliath." I took a few stimulating breaths and looked through the misted windshield and deluge, at the stone-white, pristine building, untainted after years of rain. How could it be so immaculate?

I wondered. As if anticipating my thoughts, Goliath explained.

"This temple is of a special construction, the white rock is everlasting, never staining, always clean.. It represents the, let me see, the sacredness, sanctity of the beliefs of the people here. The people that, that were here. They are no more."

"I am sorry," I said clumsily. I recovered a little when I said "I, I mean we should take thanks for stumbling into this, take hope from their building, their faith. It is a gift, I am so tired and need a place of refuge. How well preserved that building is! If this represents the people, they must have been truly remarkable. It was truly built to last."

"Yes, it is rumored that the rock takes about ten orbits just to get it out of the ground. It is only found in one place some thousand kilometers from here. These were a determined people. They looked long into the future, tried to make things for later generations. But we were not able to stop them from dying, from the short-sighted behavior of others. It is a shameful thing for my people."

I had a thought. "How far are we from our destination, our target site, Goliath?"

"Let me see. Fifty kilometers. Not far now. Maybe tomorrow."

"But does this not mean that any people in our target zone might be from this region, might descend from those who built this?"

"Yes, it could be. But, well, tomorrow is tomorrow, today is today. Let us not borrow from tomorrow."

"Yes indeed," I said, "well said." I was about to continue when we heard Terra say over the intercom,

"The sacred building will perform a sacred task again. It will take care of us tonight. Let us stop and refresh ourselves, and rest." After ten minutes out, roped together in the appalling weather, we had entered the temple, as I called it. It was like our underground village, the Cordoba Mosque but in miniature, with all kinds of nooks and crannies. Our lanterns showed brilliant white stone with very small solid-looking windows. The winds had left the building untouched, I was astonished, the glass must be like diamond. Even the noise of the weather was greatly diminished. Although exhausted, I spent a few minutes exploring the building, we had installed several standing lamps and the architecture and art interested me. The artwork was etched into the stone, as bas-relief, highlighted with jet black shading. It depicted scenes of pastoral beauty, emphasizing how the planet had nurtured the people through rich harvests, shoals of fish, herds of kine, sun and rain. I was fascinated and wandered with Colin, looking at this first glimpse of a life before the global disaster. This building knew nothing of the planetary crisis, except that the people no longer came.

"Dad, look here. This pattern, this is Orion, isn't it? See the belt? But the place with the nebula shows something different, something Wendy used to do with Peter and Barrie when they were babies." I looked over, raised my lamp, and saw a stone-cutting of a mother, breastfeeding a baby, right in the heart of the Orion nebula.

"The Nursery." I said. "Luna. I wonder if Luna's people came from here."

"What's Luna got to do with this? She's over there." He pointed at the image of a crescent moon in the constellation of Taurus. He obviously thought I was speaking of Luna, in reference to the moon. Then his expression changed to one of realization. He had obviously paid attention, great attention, during our first few days with our first Cetacean being. "Oh, I see, at least I think I see what you mean, you are talking of him, her partner, returning to The Nursery. She was saying goodbye to her partner, and she was sending him to Orion. Now she carries his babies."

I felt we were uninvited guests in a very private place, invading a private culture. "Dad, I have been reading about what prayers are. I think we should say one now, it seems right. God bless Luna, and her little ones Michael and Rosie."

"Amen," I said, with tears in my eyes. I put my arms around Colin and said, "You are really growing up Colin, I am proud of you. You understand so much more at your age than I ever did. You are the future, you and Andrea. I think your future will be very bright."

"Dad, you're not exactly dumb. You might be a nerd, but you are not dumb." We hugged and prepared for a good sleep, feeling very secure in the hands of an ancient culture.

The next day we arose to a very tempting aroma of fresh coffee. Terra had prepared a hot breakfast, and had snuck in some Earth recipes for myself and Colin. We were at an altitude where the outside temperature at night dropped to fifteen Celcius, it was pleasantly cold. The food smelled wonderful, a porridge/ dried fruit mix. With the fresh coffee and the thought of meeting one of the people who might have built this remarkable building, I felt ready to fight the winds, rain, and mud once again.

We started all three cats, and after some checks we moved out into drumming rain. Terra was navigating, Firma leading. Hours went by. The grinding of the tracks under the cats, the hum of the engine, the relentless wipers on the windows, the endless rain, and Goliath's humming of his folk tunes, had gradually sent me to sleep once again. I had suffered a little from cramps at night after two days in the cats, and although I had slept well, now was feeling quite exhausted again.

I woke up, aware of something going on outside of the hypnotic and regular noises of the cat. I felt ashamed of myself for sleeping. "Michael, wake up, wake up. You will have to move over, my friend," said Goliath, turning around and smiling. The smile was the biggest smile he could remember, right in the middle of a very small face. In front of the cats was a family. Two adults, three children, one a baby. They were emaciated, filthy, rain pouring off their makeshift ponchos. Their eyes stared at myself and Colin, they were dark, hollow circled eyes, something I had only seen in the history of our world during times of war and famine. As I looked, the female adult collapsed into a deep puddle of mud, still protecting her baby. We stepped clumsily into action. I was so much bigger than everyone else, I immediately picked up the mother, having passed the baby to the father. I carried her into the cabin of the cat. The father broke down in tears, he was escorted by Colin to another cat's refuge. He appeared at first to notice we were quite alien, but it was to him then of no consequence.

The population of the Cetacean world's people had increased by five. Out of the 62 known living souls, this was equivalent to finding a lost tribe on Earth with the population of Brazil. Each of these people had been through hell. They were survivors. These were obviously tough, determined people, we would all have much to learn from them. To me, these people were the epitome of Wendy's words. *Credo ergo sum.*

As a scientist I also knew that each new combination of DNA meant a dramatic increase in the chances of long-term survival of our new friends' species. We quickly did what we could to dry our precious cargo and boarded the cats. We were cramped, but warm, and we would all dry out eventually. Our new guests were immediately fed fresh bread, and hot soup. They all feel asleep. I tried to imagine what they had been through, as we turned about, and headed for the white temple again.

It rained harder than ever, the wind picked up, we could hear thunder and then the roar of a tornado somewhere. Colin said "Dad, this is a good day, a very good day indeed," over the intercom. Those familiar drumming, whining, blowing and grinding sounds were among the happiest sounds I could remember, ever.

Made in the USA
San Bernardino, CA
07 June 2016